BY LIGHT
WE KNEW
OUR NAMES

BY LIGHT
WE KNEW
OUR NAMES

ANNE VALENTE

DZANC
BOOKS

DZANC
BOOKS

5220 Dexter Ann Arbor Rd.
Ann Arbor, MI 48103
www.dzancbooks.org

Some of these stories appeared in the following places in slightly different forms:

"Latchkey," *Berkeley Fiction Review*, 2011; "Dear Amelia," *Copper Nickel*, 2012; "To a Place Where We Take Flight," *Storyglossia*, 2009; Dzanc Books *Best of the Web 2010*; "Terrible Angels," *Surreal South Anthology*, 2011; "A Taste of Tea," *Midwestern Gothic*, 2012; "Everything that Was Ours," *Freight Stories*, 2011; "By Light We Knew Our Names," *Hayden's Ferry Review*, 2011; "If Everything Fell Silent, Even Sirens," *Sou'wester*, 2012; "A Very Compassionate Baby," *Annalemma*, 2010; Notable Story, *Best American Non-Required Reading 2011*; "Minivan," *Bellevue Literary Review*, 2011; "Not for Ghosts or Daffodils," *The Journal*, 2013; "Until Our Shadows Claim Us," *CutBank*, 2012; "Mollusk, Membrane, Human Heart," *Memorious*, 2012.

Designed by Steven Seighman

Library of Congress Cataloging-In-Publication Data is available upon request.

ISBN: 978-1-936873-62-3

First edition: September 2014

Printed in the United States of America

10   9   8   7   6   5   4   3   2   1

For my parents
with gratitude and love

CONTENTS

LATCHKEY

Sasha's birthday fell on a Wednesday, and though her parents gave her a present, its string and paper meant to be torn away at once, almost ten days have passed and still she has not opened it. They wrapped it in paisley paper, tied a bright purple string around its corners, and hoped she would pull all the casings away, just after she blew out the seven candles on her frosted yellow cake. But when Sasha blew hard across the sugared flowers, her cheeks puffed like globes, her mother made her close her eyes, placed the gift in her hands; and when Sasha opened them and looked down, she only said *I love it*, her voice a low whistle, and set it aside on the carpet fully wrapped.

Don't you want to open it? her mother asked.

But Sasha said no, and her mother looked at her father over Sasha's small head, then Sasha said it again, that she loved it as it was, and her father cut the cake and gave his daughter the corner piece, the one with the most frosting, as she always liked.

They might have thought something was wrong, that maybe she anticipated what it was and knew she wouldn't like it, and refused to expose her disappointment there in the kitchen, in front of her parents and the candle smoke drifting in curls toward the ceiling. But after Sasha ate her cake, she bent down and picked up the present and clutched it tight against her chest as her parents led her to the car to take her to the movies. She brought it with her into the theater, an animated feature she'd wanted to see for weeks, and after the credits rolled and they drove their daughter home, Sasha carried the present into her bedroom and pulled it under the covers with her, gripped it like a stuffed animal as she fell asleep.

And now, almost two weeks later, Sasha still will not open her gift, even though she carries it everywhere like a lucky charm. Her parents have asked her, delicately at times, if maybe she wants to open it, maybe see what's inside. But she shakes her head no each time, grips the paisley edges tighter, and the whites of her knuckles have made her parents stop, have told them there is no more need to ask.

Sasha sits on the playground at recess, one arm holding the present, the other gripping a wood chip that she digs into the soft dirt until a pill bug rolls out. It lies curled up, playing dead, and Sasha puts down the wood chip and pokes it, prodding gently. The bug unfurls and crawls away and she watches it go, hard back glistening in the afternoon sunlight. A shadow passes overhead and Sasha squints up to see who is standing over her.

What are you doing? Ben asks. He sits next to her in class, builds soda-bottle terrariums alongside her, condensation beading like raindrops inside the bottles' plastic walls.

Looking up, Sasha can't see his halo, always hidden when other people are around.

I don't know, she says.

He looks at her wood chip, then at the present clutched under her arm.

Why don't you just open that?

It's fine as it is, she says, and pulls it tighter against her side.

Ben sits down next to her, picks up a wood chip of his own.

Well, what do you think it is? he asks, and when he looks at her she sees Saturn glinting in his eye, so small no one else can see it.

Maybe it's an army, Sasha sighs, and pierces the dirt with her wood chip. A tiny army of lop-eared rabbits.

Ben doesn't laugh, as maybe her parents would have. Instead Ben's eyebrows arch and his mouth bends into a smile.

Travis and Jane are both going today, he says. Maybe you can open it then.

Sasha smiles, holds her mouth in a curve as Ben walks away. But when he's gone she looks down and digs, and wonders if there will ever be a right time to open it, if it will ever be as perfect as it is now.

After school Sasha rides the bus to Ms. Carraway's house, the woman in her neighborhood who watches her until her parents come home from work, who watches lots of other children in the neighborhood too, including Ben, Travis, and Jane. Travis and Jane are a year older, and it's only at Ms. Carraway's that she sees them, and even then only some days, the days no parent can pick them up from school. Though Ms. Carraway sometimes watches up to ten children at once, they always seem to go home before Sasha and Ben and Travis and Jane. When just the four of them are left, Ms. Carraway puts on a movie for them and naps, slinks back into her bedroom like a cat until the doorbell rings and it's time for them to start going home. It was during a movie that Sasha first discovered it, that she was the only one not like them.

They were watching *Beauty and the Beast*, Sasha curled up on the floor while Ben and Travis sat on the couch, Jane in a beanbag chair nearby. Sasha leaned back for a handful of Chex Mix and noticed a halo of planets orbiting Ben's head, spinning like children on a merry-go-round. Sasha gasped, dropped the Chex Mix on the carpet, and Ben glanced at her, unconcerned. Jane and Travis also looked unfazed, kept watching the movie, and that's when Sasha discovered they all had secrets, and she was the only one without something special, some small mystery to call her own.

Today there are three other children, seven in total, and Ms. Carraway feeds them cookies and lets them play board games—Battleship for Sasha, her favorite since kindergarten, and Ms. Carraway is kind enough not to ask about the present, which rests unopened in Sasha's lap. But once the others go home, parents arriving in the doorway and escorting their children to the car, Ms. Carraway corrals the remaining four into the living room and puts on a movie. *Back to the Future* this time, since they say they are tired of cartoons.

Ms. Carraway escapes to her bedroom, and when the door shuts, the planets appear around Ben's head like a crown. Travis's round belly becomes a fishbowl, full of puffers, jellyfish, a hermit crab perched on a rock. And Jane laughs and whispers into her pocket, where a small librarian tickles her with his wiggling movements, his voice so small it sounds like a squeak, but a squeak that can recount encyclopedia entries on request.

Sasha sinks into the couch cushions, sloping into their safety, and clutches the present against her shirtfront, hoping the others won't notice her. But Ben remembers, climbs across the couch toward her, and sits on the middle cushion on his knees, looking at her. Sasha watches Mars spin on its tiny axis above him, small between Earth and Jupiter, the latter the size of a grapefruit.

Hey, now you can open it, Ben says, eyes moving to the package.

Yeah, why not? Jane says. The librarian pokes his head out of her pocket and nods too.

Sasha looks at Jane and Ben, then Travis, who isn't watching them, eyes cast down upon a seahorse, fins whirring, small body propelling itself around his fishbowl.

I don't know, Sasha says, and looks down at the present, at its paisley print and bright purple ribbon. She hugs it tighter, holding it close like a newborn.

Don't you want to know what's inside? Travis says absently, eyes still on the seahorse, which has whirred its way to the front of his glass belly and looks out at them.

I want to know, the librarian squeaks from Jane's pocket, so softly Sasha can barely hear him.

But as Sasha looks down at the gift, the wrapping paper stretched like thick skin across its edges, a shudder pulses through her at the thought of the paper being ripped away, as if skin itself would be torn and split.

Well, I don't, she says. It's fine the way it is.

The fabric of Jane's pocket moves, small stabbing darts, as if the librarian is punching the material from inside.

I want to know! he shouts, but the movie is loud enough to drown out his tiny screams.

Ben sits back on his heels, the planets ambling across his forehead like a parade.

Well, what do you think it is? Ben asks again. What do you think, really?

Sasha sighs. It must be a carrier pigeon, she says, a diving bird that will take my wishes to the bottom of the sea and bury them safe in the ocean floor.

Ben drops into the couch cushions and smiles. But looking down at the package, Sasha doesn't believe what she's said. She doesn't know if it is anything more than paisley paper and string, but, she thinks, she wouldn't be unhappy if that was all it was.

After dinner, Sasha watches television in the living room with her parents. Her mother works on a crossword puzzle at one end of the couch, and Sasha sits on her father's lap at the other end. He reads a book over her head while she watches the screen, the present lying across her belly.

Sasha, sweetheart, her mother sighs, it's been two weeks. She bites her lower lip and doesn't look up as she speaks, pen scribbling against the newspaper. Sasha turns back to the television, slumps lower on her father's lap.

Don't you want to open it? her mother says. Aren't you tired of carrying that around?

What she is tired of is people asking. The weight of the present, it feels like nothing more than the weight of butterfly wings. It is a weight she could carry indefinitely.

Well, we never did throw you a birthday party, her father says. He peers over his book at Sasha, who is already looking up at him, her eyes big. Why don't some of those friends of yours come over? The ones that are always at Ms. Carraway's with you.

Sasha tenses, her muscles retreating like turtles into shells, so solidly she thinks her father must feel her twitches through his shirtsleeves. But he just peers down at her and smiles, asks, What do you think?

Sasha looks down at her present, nods so softly it could almost be a no, then slides off her father's lap and climbs the stairs to her room, crawling into the covers with her package clutched tight, as though it might disappear.

After school the next day, Ms. Carraway puts on *Flight of the Navigator* and retreats to her bedroom for a nap. Sasha sits with the others on the couch and keeps her eyes on the television. The paisley gift sits like a lapdog on her knees. She pretends not to watch the others, their acrobatic magic.

My parents are throwing me a birthday party, Sasha says, so casually it hurts. They want all of you to come.

Jane leans forward, the librarian perched on her shoulder.

Will there be cake? she asks. The librarian smiles, tells the room some cakes include cream of tartar.

I think so, Sasha says. Soda and chips too.

When is the party? Travis asks. She can't see his face, since he's on the other end of the couch, but his glass belly protrudes almost to the edge of the cushions. Today a tiny octopus keeps squeezing itself in and out of a ring-shaped rock.

Saturday afternoon at my house, Sasha says. We'll play pin the tail on the donkey. Maybe more board games. I have Battleship too.

It sounds like fun, Jane says. The librarian nods and claps, peeps in his small voice that parties are often accompanied by balloons and streamers.

So is Saturday when you're finally going to open that? Ben asks. He leans forward, points at the gift. His planets aren't rotating today; Saturn sits like a Frisbee disc at the back of his head.

I don't know, Sasha sighs. She looks down at the gift, instinctively pulls it close, though even she, she too, is beginning to wonder if just opening it would be easier.

Well, I want to know what it is, Ben says, and when he speaks, Sasha realizes that she does too, almost as badly as everyone else in the room. But when she looks down at the package, at its paisley edges and purple string, she wonders if what lies beneath could possibly be better than those colors, that pattern, if what's known is ever better than what isn't.

Ben sits back, and Sasha worries for a moment that his head might crush Saturn against the couch cushions.

Well, maybe Saturday is perfect, Ben says. Your parents will be there, and so will we.

Sasha isn't entirely sure what he means, since the three of them have only met her parents a few times. And she doesn't know why it matters whether these three are present either. They're not really even friends.

Sasha settles back into the couch, pretends to watch the movie, but what she's really watching is the octopus, compressing itself through the small ring. She thinks of her party, how strange and new it will be to have friends in her house.

At dinner that night, Sasha pours honey onto a butter knife and dips it into her pile of peas. The peas stick, clinging to the knife's flat sides, and Sasha bites the peas off one by one, the gift nearby, on the fourth chair around their kitchen table.

My friends said they're coming, Sasha says. Her mother clasps her hands together, and her father smiles, his cheeks full of mashed potatoes.

Oh, honey, how wonderful! her mother says. I'm so glad we're having a party for you.

I can get started on the pin-the-tail board, her father says. Do you want a donkey, or something else? Maybe a bronto-saurus?

Sasha looks at her dad. That'd be a pretty big tail, she says.

All the more fun! her father says, and because he's so excited, Sasha nods and eats her peas.

You know, sweetheart, you don't have to, her mother says. But maybe, if you wanted to, your present—

You could open it then, her father finishes. Her parents look at each other across the table. Sasha looks down at her plate and keeps eating her peas.

What do you think it is? her dad asks.

A sweater, Sasha says, though it's almost May, no snow for nearly two months.

Oh, surely you know we'd do better than that! her mother says.

Maybe it's a doll, Sasha says, and when she looks up, her parents seem hurt, as if she's said something wrong.

That night, as she climbs into bed, she brings the package with her. But instead of clutching it against her chest, as she's done for the past two weeks, she sets it on the pillow beside her and watches it, wishing she could see through the paper to the inside, wishing and watching until she fades to sleep.

On Saturday, after Sasha's mother has baked a new cake topped with yellow frosted daisies, and after her father has built a large poster out of cardboard, a huge brontosaurus missing the length of its tail, Sasha stands looking out the front window until at last a car pulls up. Ben arrives first, hopping out of a red Honda with a small gift, and Jane and Travis follow soon after, holding presents in their soft hands.

Sasha is surprised at first not to see the orbiting planets, the rotund fishbowl, the little librarian standing atop Jane's shoulder. But then she remembers, her parents are here, and she has never seen their tricks outside the confines of Ms. Carraway's secluded living room, or within sight of adults.

Pretty dress, Jane says, and touches the hem of Sasha's purple polka-dot skirt. Sasha blushes, and before she can say thank you, Jane steps into the family room and places her gift on the table, alongside the others Ben and Travis have brought. The paisley package is also there, stacked beneath the smaller ones, and though Sasha has kept it at a distance all morning, she eyes it as her mother greets Jane in the family room, offers her a soda, and places it in both of Jane's hands, her small fingers encircling the plastic cup.

Who wants to play pin the tail on the brontosaurus? Sasha's father asks, once they're all sitting on couches, jackets discarded, sodas fizzing and bubbling.

Ben raises his hand, alongside Travis and Jane. Sasha looks at all three of them and raises her hand too, sure now after a morning of worry that her father's idea will be a success.

He pulls four enormous cardboard tails from behind his armchair and hands one to each of them. Ben asks Sasha if she'd like to go first, since it's her birthday. But she shakes her head no, and shrinks to the back of the line, and Ben shrugs and Sasha's dad places a red bandanna across his eyes as a blindfold. He spins Ben by the shoulders, and lets the other three children help, and Ben wobbles toward the wall and pins the tail near the brontosaurus's front foot, so low that the tail looks like a tree branch the dinosaur will step over.

Jane and Travis laugh, and Ben pulls off the blindfold and grins. Sasha's mom snaps a picture of the first attempt, and she readies her camera as the others spin Jane first, then

Travis, Jane's tail landing somewhere near the dinosaur's elongated belly, Travis's resting on its head like longhorns.

There is so much laughter in the room that Sasha almost feels ready for her turn. But when her father places the blindfold soft against her eyes, she shuts them tight to blink back the possibility of tears, and with them, the slimmest of chances that she will find her way to the right spot.

But when she moves her feet ahead, unsteady beneath the tail's surprising weight, she walks only a few steps before her hands make contact with the wall. She feels for the cardboard, for the rough texture of the brown paint her father used to construct the dinosaur. She holds the tail above her head and presses it firmly against the board, and as soon as she does, the room erupts in claps and cheers.

Sasha pulls the blindfold away from her eyes, and in front of her the tail aligns in perfect symmetry with the brontosaurus's body. Her face breaks into a smile, and her friends crowd around and hug her while her mother takes pictures, and her father admires the tail she's placed upon his unfinished game board, now complete, the dinosaur intact.

Sasha's mother puts on a short cartoon for them to watch while she and Sasha's father prepare the cake in the other room. It is a birthday cartoon, Winnie-the-Pooh's special celebration, and it is only when all four children are settled into the couch cushions, eyes rapt on the television, that Sasha feels all the tension inside her start to melt away, pooling into a puddle she can almost see. Ben looks over at her, and squeezes her on the shoulder and smiles, and it is then that Sasha sees his planets begin to spin, the crown of his head glowing as if it were the sun.

Ben, your planets, Sasha whispers, and he looks over at her and smiles, I know.

But my parents—she starts to say, until she looks at Jane and Travis, and sees Jane's librarian peeking out of her shirt pocket, Travis's fishbowl illuminated to reveal a chambered nautilus ambling through the water.

But they'll see! Sasha whispers, a little louder this time before she catches herself, peeks over the back of the couch at her parents in the kitchen, who are oblivious, cutting the daisy cake.

But neither Ben, nor Jane, nor Travis respond at all. They only look at her and smile, knowing smiles that place her on the outside of what they collectively seem to know.

Winnie-the-Pooh was created by A.A. Milne, after his own son's boyhood, the librarian says, poking out of Jane's shirt pocket, his voice muffled by the fabric.

Sasha stares at the librarian. Where does he sleep at night? she can't help but ask, despite his strange smallness, despite Travis's fishbowl and the slow-moving nautilus and her parents just beyond the couch in the other room.

On a coaster on my nightstand, Jane says. He curls up and sleeps near my head.

Sasha looks at her paisley gift, sitting on the table like a silent watchman as they look past it to the television, to Christopher Robin lighting birthday candles. She doesn't know why, but she wants to know, now, what lies inside purple ribbons, beneath paisley layers.

Maybe you can open your present now, Ben says, almost as if he's read her mind, as if the planets spinning around his head have pulled her own thoughts into their gravitational orbit.

But my parents—Sasha says again before she stops herself short, as the lights in the kitchen dim, as over the couch she sees her parents approaching the living room, turning off lights as they go, the cake a glowing lantern in her mother's hands.

They begin to sing happy birthday, all of them, and Sasha watches as the fishbowl, the planets, the librarian all fail to disappear. Her parents are almost to the living room now, the cartoon muted as they all sing loudly, and Sasha finds herself tethered to the couch, unable to speak or move, terrified at what her parents will find when the few steps before them become none. Sasha stares at Ben's planets, at the small, ice-dust ring that encircles his Saturn, and in that moment her father's voice is the only one she can hear, the low baritone of it, the way it wavers slightly off key maneuvering over the notes.

Sasha's parents step into the room and lower the cake before her, and as the candles waver and bend beneath her quickened breath, and the song ends, and the room erupts in another round of claps, Sasha looks up to see that her friends' magic has not left the room, and even so, her parents have not flinched once.

Sasha looks from her parents to her friends, all of them staring at her wide-eyed, smiling. And though she doesn't understand the quick release that their expressions afford her, the way she feels her rib cage melt into itself and relax, she bows her head toward the candles and blows, extinguishing all seven candles in one cathartic breath.

Her mother begins to cut the cake, squaring off the corner piece just for Sasha, the one with the most frosting. Sasha looks at Ben's planets, the librarian leaning far out of Jane's pocket toward the cake, at a snail dragging its muscled foot across the glass of Travis's belly, and she wonders if maybe her parents just can't see them, until her father bends his face near Travis's fishbowl and taps his finger against the snail.

Big fellow there, Sasha's dad says. Ever get any turtles in here?

Sasha stares at her dad, then back at Travis. Her dad looks over at her and smiles, though he says nothing, only grabs the paisley present from the table and places it in her hands.

There is a reason you stay too, Sasha, Travis says, his hands around his fishbowl like a watermelon. And it's not because your mom and dad work late.

Sasha isn't entirely sure yet that she knows what he means, or even why he's chosen this moment to say it. But her mom stops cutting the cake and gives Sasha the same smile that her father has, and it's then that Sasha knows she'll never again carry the fully wrapped package to bed, and that now is the time she must tear away the paisley paper.

What is it? she can't help asking, even though her fingers hover over the purple ribbons, even though she could tear away the paper this second and find out for herself.

Her parents look at one another, exchange a glance Sasha can't quite decipher.

We don't know, her mother finally says. It's up to you, really.

Sasha looks down at the gift, and before she can let herself question this any more, wonder what's inside or even determine what her mother means, she rips away the ribbon and pulls back the paper, its give not like torn skin as she'd imagined but more like the give of cotton candy wisps, pulled lightly from cardboard sticks.

What lies inside, curled in a small ball beneath the box's tissue paper, is a baby giraffe, hooves dark, mouth open in a yawn, tongue outstretched and purple.

Sasha looks up at her parents, who look back at her smiling still, their faces warm, her mother reaching across the coffee table to grab the camera for more pictures. The giraffe stands on shaky legs inside the box and blinks about the room, until its long-lashed eyes settle on the smaller presents her friends have brought, and it wobbles to the table and bites through the packaging. Sasha gasps, from embarrassment or shock, until she sees that the small packages contain apples, some carrots, small portions of oats for the giraffe to consume.

We didn't know what they'd be either, Ben says, gesturing toward the half-eaten packages, his planets nearly glowing across his forehead. They're meant to help. You know, with whatever your gift ended up being.

Sasha considers the mystery of this package, beyond its strange newness, and beyond what her parents and her friends already seem to know. She looks for a moment around the room, at what her friends' secrets maybe say about them. Ben has always been good at solar sciences in her class, and Jane is her grade's best reader. Sasha doesn't know much about Travis, but thinks that he must love the ocean, all the creatures that float through its salty waters. Sasha looks at the baby giraffe jumping awkwardly around the room, licking her mother's hair and peering into Travis's glass belly, and though she desperately wishes to know, she has no idea what this small creature says about her.

But later that night, after her friends have given her hugs and gone home, after her parents have tucked her into bed and kissed her forehead and after she's finally thrown away the paisley paper, the purple string sticking out of their kitchen trash can like confetti, Sasha falls asleep with her arms encircling the giraffe's neck. The baby giraffe yawns and settles into its own separate sleep, and though Sasha still doesn't understand her new gift, its size taking up almost her entire bed, she thinks its purple tongue feels like a lullaby on her nose, soft and warm, and its height, the tallest secret she's ever wanted to keep.

DEAR AMELIA

We imagined you from the shore, our hands pulling in lobster traps, seared red by the rope. We first knew of you in proximity, all those miles of water we squinted across to glimpse the sheen of metal wings buoyed, weightless in flight. We waited always for the newspaper, our Maine coast remote and cast off from the regularity of radio waves, and felt the weight lift in our chests on the news of yours—your small fluttering heart, pounding hard above Newfoundland, tracking ceaselessly, endlessly, determinedly east.

We followed your first transatlantic flight, how you derbied from California to Cleveland. We scanned the smudged headlines for you as the July sun threw its northern heat against our backs. We dreamed of you from the restless damp of summer-soaked sheets, a heat still calming as the cold threat of war blew through our windows, drifting slowly toward our coast from the trampled soil of other lands. And we thought of you from the quiet of the docks, where we heaved in trap after trap while our fathers cast themselves out to sea, and while our mothers watched us silently from the kitchen windows, placing dishes back in cupboards. We felt their gazes bore into us, as searing as summer sun, waiting for what was ursine within us to take its slow, lumbering shape.

Our mothers sensed the war coming in the keen coil of their ears. They heard it in the low hum of easterly winds blown across our yards, rattling clotheslines, something minor and mournful, their ears pricked in animal instinct to danger, one of many secrets they kept. We saw the way they paused while passing salt shakers across the dinner table, a nearly imperceptible hiatus, and how they looked up sometimes while knitting as if they'd heard the call of a doorbell no one else detected. And then those brief lapses became long stretches of listening, disguised as daydreams so our fathers would never notice, so they'd remind our mothers only to get back to dishwashing, to stop their foolish reveries and resume the hardened pace of work.

But we knew. We knew enough to keep quiet. We knew to never tell our fathers, though we barely knew anything ourselves, and to silence the growing gauntlet within us toward what we were, though none of us wanted to know. We continued to watch the headlines. At night we stirred, awake, forcing everything from our minds but monoplanes, the glint of your tail wing fading east. And during the day, while we pulled trap upon trap from the ocean, the only work we'd ever known, we tried not to look at each lobster, at the hardened exoskeletons of their bodies and how they summoned envy from our own. To sink into the sea, to appropriate their shells. To be everything they were, calm crustaceans, instead of the inevitability of what other animal we would become.

Our mothers evaded explanation. They left truth to hearsay. We'd heard all our lives about a tribe of Maine black bears, a vicious clan hiding deep inside the woods. Part human, part ursine. Born of the same strands of American legend as the Jersey Devil, as Blackbeard's ghost upon the shore. We'd told their tale to each other as children and scared ourselves to sleep while mirages of claws and fur whirled above our beds, the dreamed smoke of myth that dissipated at dawn. We'd heard of sightings at the misted tree line, of congregated furs so dark they appeared only as phantoms to those who'd seen them, to fishermen and hunters, to lone hikers trekking through wood.

Our parents sandboxed our play to the corners of the yard. Their eyes scanned the shadowed edge of forest beyond our neighborhoods, we always thought for wolves or for moose. Our fathers thought so too, but not our mothers, we somehow knew. In the clarity of hindsight, we remember their glances, the way their eyes slid away. We remember how they packed up picnic dinners early, cleared sweating glasses of sun tea from the table, put away plates and forks as the sun splintered at the tree line and sank slowly into the woods. We remember our early bedtimes, being tucked in well before the hushed sky broke its own silence with stars. We remember how on the nights when we couldn't sleep and crept down the hall for a glass of water, we saw our mothers standing at the windows watching the woods, their arms wrapped tightly across their chests as if to gate themselves inside.

We first intuited what we were as we watched your first solo flight, your Lockheed Vega wavering through ice and wind toward the blinking lights of Paris. We held our breath as you took off from Newfoundland, 932 miles to our north-east according to our fathers' nautical maps, and we felt the distance between our two coasts collapse, your pioneered path mirroring the shaken ground of our own. As your single-engine plane skyrocketed steadily over the ocean, we too charted new territory, a shuddering stretch beyond our bounds, a secret we guarded closer than blood.

Our bodies were changing, in ways we never expected. We'd learned in middle school of breast growth, of height spurts, hormones that sprouted unwanted hair. We recognized the discarded wads in the girls' bathroom, wrapped in toilet paper and stained darker than mud. We overheard our classmates' quiet discussions outside the earshot of boys, of how their mothers had bought them training brassieres, how they knew not to wear white skirts to school. These were things we expected, changes we'd learned would come. But we didn't anticipate the coarse brown hair growing steadily up our midline, across the once-smooth skin of our bellies and chests. We leveled ourselves confused in our own mirrors, sidled close to the reflection, and pried our lips open to inspect our growing teeth, sharp points we concealed in the school cafeteria by chewing with our mouths closed. We kept nail files in our backpacks, just like every other girl, but we concealed our hands beneath our desks and whittled away while our teachers spoke, at fingernails that grew into harsh, razored peaks no matter how vigorously we scraped. We rejoiced when our periods at last came, the mottled red of our panty lines a blemish to keep, some talisman to hold that we were normal like everyone else. But when they came only once and dried up, when we realized the following spring that an unexpected stain would blot our clothes just once each year, we locked the secret tight and lied in the locker room, laughed and complained with the other girls about unwanted spots and stockpiled rags. At home we shaved our chests in the privacy of the shower, hair that always grew back, and we never thought to ask our mothers why, our cheeks scarlet with a metronome pulse of shame.

We watched you with hope, Amelia, that your journey somehow paralleled ours. That you set off for Paris and landed in Ireland, so far afield from what you'd imagined, a foreign terrain that must have looked strange to you when you at last stepped from the plane. We consumed the headlines, the small print detailing your unanticipated trajectory, and our chests pounded the solidarity of transference that in the end, your path still kept you safe.

We followed your feats, your stunts and races. Our bodies drifted from middle school to high school, expanded into lockered corridors and musty classrooms, and all the while we kept ourselves guarded. We changed in gym class after other girls had left, trading tardiness to our next classes for unashamed solace, and some of us even took our nail files to teeth, tried to grind our incisors down to rounded stubs. We glued our gaze to the printed word of your flights from Honolulu to Oakland, from Los Angeles to Mexico City, landscapes we'd never see but imagined as sun-tinted and bright, a warm glow from the west that washed a calm over our coast. We considered what the ocean would look like at sunset and not sunrise, an orange disk sinking into the cool black rather than rising from hazed ash. We continued to pull in lobsters after school, sometimes in the gray morning of before, and at times imagined our hands encircled not around braided rope, but around the thin curve of a steering wheel as our cockpit rose in flight.

And then the headlines changed, as gradually as your ascents. We began to learn the terse details of your first around-the-world flight, smaller spots alongside larger stories of invasions and civil wars, those headlines blared in deeper black. Our mothers read alongside us, over coffee before we left for class, then over our shoulders after school when we took breaks from the docks, when we came inside for water and flipped through the papers still scattered across the table. They said nothing but we felt them waiting—for what, we didn't know. But as we returned to the docks and pulled in more traps, we felt our hands leave the rope and slide wistfully over the shape of each lobster, the glean of hard backs so unlike our furred chests.

And then that spring, snow still blanketing our town as the equinox came and went, your plane shuttled toward its first attempt around the world and ground-looped, immediately, in Pearl Harbor. We saw grained images of the plane spinning in tight circles, a cyclone across the runway before you ever took flight. The associated press speculated a blown tire, collapsed landing gear, possibly pilot error. We raged inside ourselves at the reporters, at the suggestion that you were at fault, that you, a pioneer, a lone diamond among shale, could err. We knew you as human, as fallible as any, but that there were no mistakes in windows slim as these, for you or for us. As your flight was called off, your plane shipped back to Burbank, we blistered our hands raw against the rough-worn rope. We sank traps back to sea, threw lobsters in bins, watched how their antennae mapped the shape of unfamiliar ground. Some of us even stopped shaving our chests over the span of days when your news no longer appeared, because what was the point, in the end, of ignoring an inevitability, a window closed.

While we still mourned, all of us watching the sky like fools for your plane to somehow appear, the Germans bombed Guernica, their involvement in Spain resounding from headlines. It was a development we might have ignored, through our sorrow and through our rage, if we hadn't noticed how our mothers shifted. We watched them scan the headlines and sit still as death, alone at the kitchen table while our fathers trawled the Eastern seaboard for mackerel and pollock, lobster season at last drawn to a close. We noticed how they raised their faces to the air, as if detecting a scent other than the lingering aroma of toast and maple syrup. Then we watched them walk outside in their robes and stand knee-deep in snow to stare spellbound toward the eastern coast, behavior we might have forgiven if they hadn't slapped us awake in our beds that night, hadn't pulled us outside, hadn't thrust us still nightgowned toward the woods.

It is time, they told us.

For what, none of us asked.

We stood in a circle at the woods' edge, far from our winter-silenced neighborhoods, our feet tattle-taling our path through the snow behind us. Our mothers stood across from us at the tree line, none of them with coats, an exodus born of urgency and secrecy though none of our fathers would be home for days.

You know what you are, they told us, an admission that left some of us white-hot with rage. That this was the first vocalized acknowledgement, out in isolated dark and bitter wind. That we'd spent years shaving hair and filing down sharp nails, all while our mothers noticed, all without comfort they might have given. But our rage was fleeting; we felt it melt down into terror, then into wonder as the reason they'd shoved us outside began to take shape.

We watched our mothers transform before us.

We watched them sink to their robed knees, dig their hands into snow.

We watched their fingers extend to claws, their backs arch, their bedclothes split under the strain as their bodies thickened, sprouted heavy fur. We watched their torsos expand into muscular cages. We watched them unfurl their mouths over fangs, their noses elongate, their faces pull into the cone of snouts. We witnessed their stretching and bulking and lengthening and solidifying until they hunched sturdy before us on all fours, a clan of Maine black bears, a legend made real, everything we'd believed as girls.

You knew, they told us. You've always known.

We wanted to run. We wanted to turn and escape across the threshold of our doorsteps, to climb inside soft sheets, to burrow into the shelter of restless, kicking dreams. But we knew they were right. We knew what we'd ignored. We glanced back at the blinking streetlamps of our neighborhood streets and watched them become an imaginary haven, haloed over homes that would never be the same for us again.

The world is changing and it's time, they told us. We are doing this for you.

They told us a war was coming. A war they could hear and smell, a war that permeated their sleep, that billowed ceaselessly across the coast on the steady beat of waves, portending only sorrow and heartbreak. They told us our fathers would go, gone so much longer than their days at sea. That all of them would go, that some of them would never come back. They told us the world should have held promise for us, that without the war things might have been different. But with the world as it was and what it was about to be, we would become factory workers instead, replacing our fathers, replacing every man in America until our lives were nothing of what they might have once been.

You will den, they told us. We will teach you.

We would go underground before the war began, we would hibernate the war away. We would evade the disquiet of daily life in a battling nation, the possibilities of invasion and famine and toil. Our mothers held a line against the woods, their downy bulk our guard. We eyed them wearily, what we would become. We tried to summon gratitude, this loopholed fate, the only protection they knew to give us. But we thought of you instead, Amelia. Your canceled flight. We imagined your plane rising over the silence of our snow-covered coast, remote in height, lost to us at last.

Our fathers returned, set out to sea again. Their trips grew longer as the spring spread its warmth, heat rising by slow degree. Our mothers packed coolers and watched them go, their boats receding to dark points on a fogged horizon, and when they at last disappeared our mothers turned back to us, told us to prepare ourselves for work. Not the work we'd known, all these years after school. Work of another kind, work we hesitated to begin.

But it began without us, regardless of want. At school we felt our hair thickening beyond our chests, climbing down our legs as we sat uncomfortably in class. We felt our soles wrinkle as we took geometry tests, our skin leathering inside our shoes, toughening into pads that bore our growing weight. Our cheeks burned a humiliated furnace when in the cafeteria we laughed at other girls' jokes, and instead of giggles we spewed snorts or unaccustomed growls. And in gym, when our classmates intercepted basketballs and pucks, we felt ourselves blaze with a new defensiveness, an irrationality we kept in check on walks home by brushing our bodies against trees, by dragging our sharpened nails against bark when we were certain no one saw.

After school we pulled in lobsters, even as the season waned and replenished itself, and even as we knew our work was futile, work we'd learned long before we could spell our names. Work borne of habit and heritage, to sustain us for life if we'd wanted, but for us, a way station until we found our own paths. A cause to sit against the docks, to watch the sky, to dream of what the world held for us and not a shortened sentence, our answer given, a finite term laid before us as our bodies unfurled inevitably toward their end. We threw lobster after lobster into bins and tried to ignore their quiet calm. We tried not to notice that in every batch we found several molting, their own inevitability of growth. Against our wills and our own hardened exteriors, we took extra care of those that molted. We sank to the baseboards of the docks, our coats shielding our growing bulk against early spring wind, and we held their changing, rigid bodies against our chests. We fingered the cracks of exoskeletons splitting down their backs, how they would soon crawl from their old shells. We knew their molting sustained them, a renewal across years and years that would keep them vital and always vulnerable. Their lifespan made us wistful, and the guilt of what we'd caught and thwarted. We felt our palms linger across their bodies, to channel the life left within them, before we placed them back into bins and made our hands let go.

Then at night, when the last glowing squares of our neighbors' windows finally burned out, our mothers led us deep into the woods. We watched them split from seam, a transformation we'd anticipated through class and work, a duality of shapeshifting that we too would soon know, they said, once we'd learned control. We wondered what our mothers' first metamorphoses must have felt like as we watched them sink down to their wild, creatured form.

We were to learn the basics. To hunt, to hide. To keep ourselves cloaked, to stay awake through the night. Everything else we'd learn through the span of years we were underground. We wanted to ask how long, if we'd bury ourselves forever, and if anyone would miss us while we hid away from the world. But we feared the answers. We feared our mothers. We feared their fangs and sharp claws, the way their bodies so easily gave way to the animal inside them. We feared their unfathomable span of secrecy, how they'd walled us out from our future and how they'd screened us from motherly instinct, how they'd never thought to protect us from their own fate. As readily as we felt twinned to them, even more, we felt lost to them. We watched their ursine bulk grow within the woods, and we watched what was human in them drain away, their eyes as cold as the empty sky above us.

Each night we learned to climb, our nails latched to bark. We learned to scale pines to search for food, and also to hide if ever our dens failed us. We learned to gather leaves and hollow out trenches. We learned to hunt, which some of us feared, the thought of tearing flesh from bone too mammalian to bear until our mothers demonstrated for us how to forage, how to seek grasses and berries, how we'd rarely need meat. We scavenged for nuts and growing spring buds, their roots sprouting from the forest floor through melted, dirty snow. We dug our hands into the open knots of trees for scuttling beetles and nests of honeycomb, our fingers moving gingerly forward to avoid stings though coarse hair had grown across our knuckles, obstructing stingers from open skin. Some of us even learned to fish in the open country's glacial lakes, the pale moon glinting from their surfaces, so smooth we feared their depths. Though we'd grown up as children of the sea, so many of us had never learned to swim. We stood at the edge of the moon-spackled shore and felt our mothers push us in, the quickest lesson. We expected our limbs to flail, our lungs to fill, until we felt our muscles move by memory. Our nails clawed through the fluid water, our leathered feet kicking, and some of us even grew smug and breached the surface to dive down deep, to seek the bottommost salmon hiding well beneath the moon's faint light.

We felt our bodies put on weight, our clothes stretched to their seams. We felt our heartbeats slow and our eyes sharpen in range. We lost our need to squint at the blackboard from the desks lining the classroom's back walls, seats we slid into knowing we would sleep, our eyes growing heavier as the spring lengthened the span of each day. Sometimes sound prevented us from sleep, every mumble or cough a shuddered blast, and sometimes we couldn't concentrate on exams even if we tried, the scratches of our teachers' idle grading too loud to endure while we worked, their pen marks as piercing as gunshots.

We held our secret close as our bodies morphed. We wore baggy clothing, long sleeves, attire unnoticed and still appropriate to the lasting spring cold. But we withdrew, found ourselves sitting with only each other at the cafeteria tables, away from the watchful glances of our peers, who would notice the way our lunches had shifted, bologna sandwiches on bread traded away for grass and honey. We slid into routine. We sat through classes, we maintained appearance. We tried to hold fast to geometry proofs and Civil War lessons, as futile now as the work we continued after school, our lobster traps full, our rope whittled down to replacement by the sharp points of our nails.

We might have accepted this, Amelia. We might have grown to love our double lives the way our mothers learned to accept theirs, all the secrets they kept, a power they held against bone, a protected full-house hand. We could have let go of our dreams on the steady beat of nocturnal lessons, bartering cockpits for hunts, swapping a blue world for the keenest sight we'd ever known. We admired our limbs, covered in thick hair but swifter than we could have imagined, gliding smoothly through lake water beneath a night sky we floated on our backs to watch. An empty sky—a sky we once gazed upon for the fluttering flash of your plane. But a sky aching and lovely in silent ether, a star-splashed beauty we could have sought again and again across so many isolated winter nights.

But then we saw your headlines, sometime in May, when late spring finally let go its grip, when the last of the lingering snow finally melted. We saw there would be a second attempt, that your plans weren't foiled. We saw that you would at last make your trip around the world, that you would take off west to east this time, that you remained steadfast and determined and would meet your goal. We read that you would take off in July, and though we didn't want them to, our hearts seized and quaked. We felt as if we would burst, and retired to our bedrooms, away from our mothers' watchful stares, our burled bodies overcome and shaking.

We felt hope for you, Amelia—a hope that had escaped us across barren nights. It took root in our chests again, against our will, in the empty spaces we'd resolved our secret would fill. But we felt ourselves come undone from you too, and from the unavoidable pull of our path. We lay upon our mattresses, too soft compared to the growing solidity of our forest dens, and felt our limbs flood with shame, at what we were, at the world beyond us that we'd so easily left behind.

————

You departed from Miami in June. Our mothers waited each day, watching out the front window for the newspaper though they already knew what headlines couldn't tell them, that a conflict was growing, that our fathers out to sea would soon be gone far longer. We waited too, our sight stealthy in perusal, of headlines of your flight and not of escalations and invasions, our glances sharp over our mothers' shoulders. We learned to hide our want from them as easily as we learned to forage for beechnuts, to lick our claws clean. We sighed our relief as the school year ended, our classmates' clothes lighter in the warming weather and ours conspicuous in length and coverage, out of season to the onset of summer. But we remained still guarded, to the talk of small towns. We heard circulated rumors of a legend resurfaced, midnight sightings of black bears along the edge of the woods. Black bears beyond the bounds of spotted wildlife, bears that seemed to transform, to disappear in mist. A congregation distinct from mammalian behavior, a clan that moved together, one that vanished at the tree line with the purpled tinge of daybreak.

We learned the dualities of our mothers, Amelia. We learned to hide our telltale bodies, to split our anatomies between daylight and moonrise. We learned their talent of circumspection, of holding two lives within us. We learned everything they wanted us to learn, and we learned it too well. We learned to shroud our animal truth from the world, and in the end, to obscure our beating hearts.

We hid our hope, Amelia, our bright burning hope that you would succeed. We knew our future and still we faltered against it, against our heightened sense of smell, our increased rate of speed. These were gifts we might have prized, if we accepted the path of our biology. But we couldn't, though we tried. We were night-dwellers meant to den, our blood coursing a line long before us. But we were girls too, girls ripped from root, girls who'd had daydreams and wishes and a place in this world. We were what we were, not only animal but human. We pulled ourselves by both poles, one born of necessity and the other of pure-bursting hope.

We drank in the fine print of your new route around the world, your plans modified by weather and global winds. We watched your plane hop from Miami to San Juan, then on to South America, then Africa to India. We imagined those continents in renewed bright image, continents separate from our forested landscape, a terrain crowding the heavens with trees. We gathered leaves and dug holes and scooped the cavities of rotting logs, and as our dens took shape we couldn't help but watch the dark wash of sky, feigning interest in the stars for your plane.

You took off from New Guinea at the start of July. A sun-drenched day, seared indelibly into our memory. We read of your twin-engine Electra, the 22,000 miles it had already covered, the mere 7,000 you had left to go. We studied the headlines and every word of small print, and we took in your photo, your flight goggles perched upon your head, your smile lit by a glow that burned within you. We remember our work that morning, how light it felt all day. How even the weight of lobster traps felt like the weight of air. We noted the size of each lobster, bigger as the weather swelled in heat, and some of us even graced the ocean with mercy for once, threw every lobster back to sea.

We were so happy for you. We knew how close you were. We knew how close we were too, to a full shift, to our precipice and our end. But that day we were weightless. We wanted to wash our light over everyone. That night we gathered twigs for dens, piled higher every leaf for full coverage, but inside us even fate felt foreign; no matter what winter we endured, you would still find your way across the water.

But in the morning, when we woke back in our beds, we found our mothers standing at empty kitchen sinks. We found them staring into fridges, sitting on unmade beds, standing at counters with half-open jars of jam. We asked them what, what was wrong, and when they wouldn't speak, we turned to the headlines.

Our newspapers lay scattered on kitchen tables, on armchairs. On footstools. On doorsteps. It doesn't matter where we found them, or that we anticipated news of war at last. What matters is what we read, and how our hearts slipped to the floor and broke.

You disappeared. Not ground-looped or steered off course, but vanished into thick mist above the ocean. We ripped through the print, every page for further news of whether you'd signaled, whether anyone heard you, whether ships had sunk their hulls to sea in order to find you, but only the briefest of reports had appeared at our doorstep, news meant to inform but nothing to ease.

We dropped the newspapers. We dropped our charade. We wanted to pull on our sea gear and fade away into the docks. But we felt our knees buckle, felt our heavy bodies sink down, not to all fours but to the haven of the soft carpet, our limbs immobile. We felt our mothers cross the floor and shake us, shout what's wrong, tell us to pull ourselves together, to get to the work that grew more and more urgent as the days tilted forward. But we couldn't move. We couldn't lift our lumbering bodies. We couldn't imagine a planet without the blinking beacons of your double engines floating above it, pulsing so far away from us but still there, we knew, so impossibly, distantly there.

We lost our fear, there on the carpet. We spun toward our mothers and finally asked them why. We tried to ask quietly. We found ourselves screaming. We emptied our long-held questions from the cavities of our lungs.

Why this, why us? Why? Why why why why why? We screamed until our voices grew hoarse, until our bodies drained away. We expected our mothers to slap us, to leave the slash of nails across our cheeks. But when we at last looked up at them, their faces appeared as stricken as ours. Their cheeks were drawn and tight, their eyes closed. They looked almost as if they were praying. We turned away, ashamed that we'd hurt them. A sorrow upon sorrow to bear. But when our eyes fell again upon the newspaper, we looked back at them, and when they wouldn't meet our glances we knew.

Our mothers, as heartbroken as us. Their empty gaze, their listless silence. We knew then that they'd watched for you too, that somewhere beneath what we'd feared in them had burned a radiating hope for a different world. We knew there was no answer, beyond our mothers, and our mother's mothers and their mothers. That this was what had always been, what they knew to do for us with the world as it was, and the undeniable threads of our blood. We wanted to ask them if we'd ever return, if there would be a time for us after every conflict had passed. But we knew at last that they didn't know, that they couldn't predict which way the war would go, what our nation would look like on the other side. We knew at last what they would have wanted to tell us. We knew at last that they dreamed.

We extended our hands to our mothers. We closed the newspapers, even though it broke us to do it. We drew ourselves from the floor and pulled our mothers up by leathered palms that matched the shape of their own.

We watched every search for you, without wanting. We read of every ship that trawled the Phoenix Islands, every naval aircraft that passed above Gardner Island. We memorized your radio transmissions, your final call. We walked gingerly around our mothers, headlines they too couldn't bear, an honesty we never reclaimed past the morning of your lost flight, a candor we never forged again. We floated through summer, an unmemorable haze. A clockwork of waking and trapping and foresting and foraging, a routine rounded dull by a vacant halo of sky. We cast our newspapers aside when official searching at last ceased. We tried to ignore the continued private searches, the growing rumors that the Pacific still held your secret.

You were declared dead this winter, Amelia. Our fathers have enlisted. After every search was at last called off, all theories debunked, our fathers cast themselves off to other shores. We are finally hiding down here in our dens. We receive no news anymore, not of war, only what winds our mothers can detect. They hold their noses to the night air, their pointed ears to light gusts. We are still learning what we need to know, but we too are building those skills.

We know you are alive, Amelia. We hold the shape of your name in our ears. You were never found, not your plane or clothing, not even the compact and lipsticks you carried in the cockpit with you. We sense your movements in the pulse of air, we feel you flow still through our veins, our burning animal blood. We watch the sky for you, from the lonesome enclave of our dens, and we wait. For this war to end. For our bodies to change. For our fathers to return, a secret they'll never know, and for the unmistakable glint of your plane above, a glint we would know as separate from stars. We wait while the lobsters grow and grow, lives we can't help but imagine, undisturbed on the floors of a silent sea. We wait to shed our thick fur, to watch our nails recede to dull moons, to whittle down our bulk and stand tall. We wait for news that they've finally found you circling the globe, a bright world beyond our cold dens, a world waiting for us when we crawl up from our knees and rise.

TO A PLACE WHERE
WE TAKE FLIGHT

In my head, it sounds better—in my head, I am Johnny Rotten screaming into a tattered microphone, I am Vince Neil shrieking to a sold-out arena, I am Roger Fucking Daltrey singing "Magic Bus" at the Monterey Pop Festival, and Chris is my Keith Moon. We play before thousands, a crowd that cheers wildly when Chris at last smashes his drum set and I throw my mike into the throngs, a ripple like a shockwave through the swarm. We sweat beneath stage lights, our skin like oil slicks, and we march offstage as the lights finally dim, as the crowd begins a slow chant—*no*, this can't possibly be the end.

It sounds better in my head.

But here, in Chris's leaky basement full of house spiders and worn carpeting, we are just two jerks, two nothings with no amps, not even a microphone, only the toy drum set Chris's dad bought him for Christmas last year. We play for no one, not even Chris's awestruck little brother, who stayed late at school for origami club—just for the basement rafters above, where the pipes leak rusty water.

But soon, we will. Not the Belmont Jr. High talent show, not Lila Duldorf's birthday party, not even the Hi-Dive down the street—things we might have once wanted, but now we have no time. Now, we're focused. We have a plan. We will play Moss Regional Hospital, something Chris's dad hooked up two days ago, because he knows a guy on the board.

We will play Moss Regional in one week. We will play to save her life.

After we practice for an hour, we grab Hi-C and Twizzlers and sit on Chris's front porch, right where we were the other day when Chris's dad came home and told us the news. Chris said right there how fucking awesome that was, and I felt like maybe I could kiss Mr. Winchester, but instead I stuffed a Warhead in my mouth and wondered why I couldn't say fuck in front of my own dad.

Though now, the real issue is that he's already given up, just sits watching the same reruns of *M.A.S.H.* and *Three's Company* over and over again while I bike to the hospital after school, or call Mom's room if I stay at Chris's too late.

"She knows we're doing this, right?" Chris bites the end off a Twizzler and looks at me.

"Sure, man, she knows. I told her last night, when we talked."

"You really think a week is enough time?"

I want to tell him we don't have any goddamn choice, but I hold my tongue and chew on my thumbnail instead.

"Jesus, Mike, don't pull that shit on my porch. If I find one of your fingernails later, I'm going to put it in your Coke when you're not looking."

In fifth grade, I'd saved a bunch of my nails and put them on Chris's pillowcase once, when we were watching *Cujo* and he got up to pee. Just for spite, I bite off my thumbnail and spit it onto the porch stairs.

"Sick, man. Better not leave your Coke unattended tomorrow at lunch."

I tell Chris he's a dick, and we sit on the porch until the Twizzlers are gone, until an ant crawls up and carries my thumbnail away.

At home during dinner, Dad is quiet. We sit in front of the television, eating microwave dinners while Nick at Nite blares from the screen, an *I Love Lucy* episode featuring Harpo Marx. Dad knows I'll call Mom when I'm finished, and I don't know whether he'll talk to her this time, or pretend to wash dishes again, though we're eating out of cardboard.

"You tell your mother about your little scheme?"

I nod, but Dad's eyes don't move from the television. He takes a bite of nuked turkey, and he smiles a little when Lucy hides behind a doorway, afraid to meet Harpo in person.

I know he thinks I'm doing this as therapy, like how music is supposed to heal, to make Mom smile—just like pets do for sick people, why tabbies live in nursing homes. Chris too, because that's what I said, when I told him I wanted to do this. But what I never told him, and what I never can, is that some part of me is doing it for that story she used to tell.

The healing is good. If nothing else, we'll have that. But why I really want this, what some small part of me still believes, is that when my voice moves across the oncology floor, filtering into her IV bag, her needles, the radiation that permeates her skin, its energy will power the tools she needs to live. And by some strange miracle—but one I can actually imagine, again and again, when I can't fall asleep some nights—the music will make her well, just like it made the ship move and fly away, the best bedtime story she ever told me.

I don't know what's made me think of that story lately, or why I even believe, in some small corner of my mind, that this will make any difference at all. She is sick, and I'm old enough now to stop believing in most things, and Dad said last week, after the doctor called and I found him standing in the kitchen, palms gripping the edge of the sink, you know, Mike, your mom might not be around forever.

But I want to believe. Even if I never tell Chris, even if he thinks we're just playing for fun, even if Dad watches reruns for the rest of his fucking life. There will still be me, my energy to hers, the last porch light, like the one she used to leave on when I was out after dark.

I wait awhile to call her, after I've done my pre-algebra homework, after I know Dad has settled into the couch for the primetime lineup, so it won't hurt so much that he doesn't pick up the phone too. They haven't been on bad terms necessarily, just distant, like maybe he doesn't know what to say to her, or like she's waiting for him to do something impossible that could make her stay on this earth.

I call directly to her room, since she's been out of surgery for a few days and the ward nurse will no longer need to mediate our calls, or make sure she's awake. She sounds groggy when she answers, like she's been taking a nap, and she tells me she's just watched *Wheel of Fortune* over a hearty dinner of Ensure.

"How is practice going? How's Chris?"

"You know, good. We can't really play with just singing and drums, though, so I borrowed Mr. Winchester's guitar."

Chris and I decided the day before that drums and vocals wouldn't be enough, so he'd asked his dad to lend me the family's acoustic. I knew a few chords from when Mom had shown me her old Bob Dylan albums, from when she told me they'd seen him live in 1972, when he was drunk as a skunk, as she'd said, and barely knew the words to his own songs. I'd borrowed her old guitar then, and learned "Blowin' in the Wind" by playing my own wobbly notes for two days against the scratch of our turntable's vinyl.

"So you remembered something from our lesson. Still listening to Bob Dylan?" Her voice brightens, and I can hear her smiling. The sound makes me want to cry.

"Nah, Mom, I've moved on. You know, Zeppelin, the Pistols. Mötley Crüe."

"I saw Led Zeppelin once, in college. I almost touched Robert Plant's shoulder after I pushed my way to the front."

The thought of her pushing anything, of having the strength to elbow through a crowd, much less leave her hospital bed, is one I can't hold onto for long.

"Mom, do you remember that story?" I blurt it out, a question I hadn't meant to bring up.

Quiet spreads across her end of the line. "What story, sweetie?"

"You know, the story. About the ship."

She's quiet again, and for a second I wonder if breast cancer has stolen her memory too, if the slow spread to her brain has blocked out everything that was once me, if maybe she doesn't even remember Dad and that's why he's been so down.

But then she laughs. "The ship in the Sea of Sadness?"

"Yes. The ship in the Sea of Sadness," I say, and something in my chest floods.

"Oh God, Mike, I haven't thought of that in so long. How do you even *remember* that?" She is laughing still, as if it's the best thing she's heard all week.

"Of course I remember. You used to tell it all the time."

"You know, that was one of your grandmother's stories. Not even mine." She is reeling. Her voice sounds drunk.

"Could you tell me again?"

"What, now?"

In her voice I hear it, that I'm too old for this now, that kids on the cusp of adolescence don't need bedtime stories anymore. If Chris were here he'd say the same thing, only he'd probably punch my shoulder and give me a dead arm, maybe call me a loser. But I tell her yes, yes I want to hear the story, now. So she tells me.

She tells me once there was a ship that sailed through the sky, a ship powered by the music of one family, a family that played flute and harp and violin and piccolo together. But one day a great storm raged through the clouds, blowing the whole family except the little boy clear away to the other side of the world, and the ship fell to the earth without any music to guide it. When the boy awoke after the storm, he was alone in a great desert of sand, on the deck of the abandoned ship, his violin broken beside him. He cried so much that the sand flooded with tears, an ocean from that day known as the Sea of Sadness.

Mom pauses a moment, like maybe she's forgotten the rest. But then she tells me that a great blue heron heard the boy's cries and flew across the Sea of Sadness, landing on the deck where the boy lay weeping. The heron pulled several strands from its own feathers and strung them across the broken violin, and when the instrument had been repaired, the bird handed it to the boy and flew away. The boy watched the heron take flight, then picked up the violin and played until the abandoned ship shuddered to life. He played the ship across the Sea of Sadness, the music conducting the boat toward his family. At last he found them, washed up on a sandy bank of deserted beach, and there they at last took flight, the ship at full speed as the family played together once more.

She tells the tale with precision, as if no time has passed between the last time she told it, while tucking me in, and now, relaying words across telephone wires. She asks, "Is that the one you meant?"

And I tell her yes, Mom, that's exactly the one.

I keep a hand over my Coke at lunch, just in case Chris remembers what he said about the fingernail. But he seems too distracted to remember, making plans for our afternoon practice, talking so fast that bits of potato chip fly from his mouth.

"Oh, and I mentioned the show to Lila Duldorf. Just in case she wants to come."

"Jesus, Chris, it's for patients. Do you really think she'll give a shit?"

"I can get her in. You know, VIP passes."

"To a fucking hospital?"

"Hey, man, simmer down. You're not the only one performing."

I look at Chris and see my mistake in not telling him. The show is a spotlight for him, nothing more.

"Fine, whatever. Invite her. Woo her with your magic."

Chris crushes a potato chip, drops the crumbs in my Coke.

In science class we talk about kinetic energy, how molecules rotate and vibrate, their electrons bumping into each other until friction causes movement. And for a second I consider this, how sound makes similar vibrations, wavelengths traveling across a room with enough energy to power cities. I scribble a drawing in my notebook, a guitar blaring notes into a stick figure's heart, and shove the picture to the bottom of my bag when the sixth period bell rings.

After school Chris and I are walking across the parking lot, heading past the lined-up school buses toward Chris's house, when Scott Barnstone comes up. He's wearing a giant pair of headphones and his hair hangs down into his face.

"Hey, I hear you guys are playing the hospital."

"Fuck off, Barnstone." Chris has never liked Scott, not since they were in after-school Latchkey together in the fourth grade and Scott spat on him once from the top of the slide.

Scott looks at me. He doesn't like me either. I accidentally clipped him once on a high-sticking penalty during gym class, when I was the goalie and he tried to check me against the net. He had a shiner for three days.

"Is it because your mom's got cancer in her tits?"

He grins at me, a line of crooked teeth. Before I can think to say anything, Chris shoves Scott in the chest.

"You kiss your boyfriend with that mouth?" Chris says, and spits on Scott's tattered sneakers. "Go back to your sandbox, Barnstone."

I tell Chris we should go. That he shouldn't say shit like that. I pull him toward the baseball fields, which we'll cross to the tree line and Chris's house.

"Whatever, assholes," Scott says. "At least I'll still have a mom after you douchebags are done playing your stupid songs."

Before I fully hear him, I drop my backpack and punch him in the face. His headphones clatter to the pavement, and I stand just long enough to see a line of blood dribble down his chin before Chris pulls me toward the fie. off, we are running.

When I get home later, the television is silent and Dad stands in the kitchen over a pot of Kraft macaroni and cheese. Two bowls on the table, two tall glasses of milk.

"I thought I'd make dinner tonight," he says. He looks up from the pot, where he's stirring the noodles and cheese powder, and smiles at me.

I leave my bag in the living room, next to Mom's old guitar. Chris and I planned to practice at least twice more before Saturday, but I'd also gotten out Mom's old acoustic and squeezed in some extra prep at home.

"So how was the day?" Dad asks when we sit down. He drops two big spoonfuls of fluorescent noodles into my bowl.

"Not great. I punched a kid in the face."

The words feel awkward, as if Dad and I don't have that ease between us anymore. Before any of this happened, he took me to the movies for whole afternoons as if he had nothing but time, and when my T-ball coach robbed me of a run, he told me my swing deserved a homer.

"He said something bad about Mom," I say.

Dad looks up from his bowl. "You shouldn't punch people."

I expect him to be mad, but he looks more hurt than anything. I take a gulp of milk and ask him about his day instead.

"You know, same old, same old. I visited your mother, though. I left work a little early."

What Dad does during the day has never really occurred to me, and when I hear him say this, I wonder for the first time if he's done this more than once. I picture him eating a sandwich alone at his desk, driving to the hospital, sitting by Mom's bed.

"Mike, there's something we need to talk about."

He sets down his fork and looks at me. His lips are thin, a pencil mark.

"Your mother—well, I talked to her doctor today. And Mike, it just doesn't look good."

He stops talking and holds his breath, and I wonder for a second if maybe he's trying to hold back a burp. But then he looks at me, and I know he's trying not to cry.

"The surgery didn't do any good. And the chemo, well, it's not doing any good either. They say it just keeps spreading."

I've only seen my dad cry once in my life, last year when we buried Sampson, the cat my parents adopted after they got married. We laid him in a shoebox and Dad dug a hole in the backyard. Two tears slid down his nose when he pushed the shovel into the ground.

"I just wanted you to know," Dad says, and I don't know what to say so I just keep eating my macaroni. He's not crying exactly, but he sits for a few more seconds without moving, then he picks up his fork and we finish the last of our dinner without talking.

That night I don't call Mom, and I don't do my homework. But before bed I set my alarm to wake up early and gain back the time I've lost doing nothing all night when I could have been practicing. It takes me a while to fall asleep, but when I finally do, it's because I've made myself think of molecules, vibrations, the passage of ships.

On Friday, the night before the show, Chris and I sit on his roof and look out toward the football field. Two teams play a scrimmage game, some peewee league sponsored by our junior high, but we watch the players dart across the field anyway, their helmets gleaming in the floodlights.

"Barnstone's face is kind of fucked up." Chris exhales a cloud of Pall Mall smoke, the pack he stole from his dad's sock drawer. It's the second time I've seen him smoke, something he must think rock stars do.

I shrug, and neither of us speaks for a while. We watch a small crowd cheer on the field's metal risers, and I wonder if those are parents, siblings, moms rooting for their sons.

"You know, I think we're ready." Chris flicks his glowing cigarette off the roof. "You don't have to worry."

I know he's right. We've been practicing all night, not even taking a break for dinner. But now, looking out across the field at the tree line just beginning to brown and fade, I wonder if we're not ready at all, if maybe we never were.

"Your mom's going to be fine," Chris says, the first time I've ever heard him say it. But he avoids my eyes, assures only because he should. "How's she doing, man? You never really talk about her."

Chris's face looks strained, as if he wants to say more. But he doesn't, and I tell him she's fine, and we sit for a while without talking. Out on the field a whistle blows, and we watch the players huddle in for halftime.

"Do you ever wonder if something totally crazy could happen?" I stare out toward the field, away from Chris.

"What, like Lila suddenly falling in love with me?" Chris laughs. "Sure, man, I wonder all the time."

"No, I mean something ridiculous," I say. "Something totally unreal."

"Playing lead with the Crüe? I think about shit like that, sure."

Chris pulls another cigarette from his stolen pack, and my chest suddenly feels heavy. I think of Dad, probably sitting in his armchair watching the Friday lineup alone, and I tell Chris I should head home, get some sleep.

Chris stays up on the roof to finish his cigarette and maybe watch the start of the second half, though neither of us cares about the game. I bike the five blocks to my house and for the first time the night air feels bitter, like autumn has arrived sooner than I thought.

We arrive at Moss Regional an hour early, but there are patients already seated and waiting, maybe some of Mom's friends from her floor. The ward has arranged chairs in a horseshoe pattern in a small lounge just past the floor's elevators, and my dad helps us set up the tiny drum set, Mr. Winchester's guitar, even a microphone the hospital's chapel let us borrow. Once everything is in place, Dad leaves us alone, says he knows we need time to prepare. I watch him head down the hallway toward Mom's room. Maybe they need time to prepare too.

"So I don't see Lila," Chris says. The room has started filling up, and I'm glad I don't recognize anyone from school.

"It's for patients, Chris. What did you expect?" Though I don't have to look at him to know we've expected different things. I tell him we can schedule another show, another time, somewhere people will actually want to go. Someplace he can shine, I think, but I stop short of saying that.

Just then I see Dad down the hallway, wheeling Mom toward us and the lounge. She looks tired, and I know she's too weak now to stand. But for some reason I think of her pushing her way toward Robert Plant, and I think of her laugh when she told me the story again on the phone, and suddenly she looks so pretty. A memory floods me from nowhere: second grade, my Cub Scout leader telling everyone I'm too short to ride horseback on the trail. Mom escorted me to the next meeting, told him I'd do anything I damn well pleased.

"Oh, sweetheart, you look great," she says when they reach us, and I bend down to hug her. Chris hugs her too and she pats his head, like she's trying to absorb the light reflected in his hair.

"You two ready?" she asks, and she smiles extra big, like something in her face might crack if she doesn't.

Chris nods, but then his dad steps off the elevator and he leaves us, just Mom, Dad, and me. For a second none of us speak. I scan my brain for something to say.

"I can't tell you how much this means to me," Mom says. She gestures toward the others gathered in the horseshoe of chairs, as if the show means something to them too, but she doesn't say anything more. Just then the head of the oncology ward waves me over, and Mom and Dad move to the edge of the horseshoe, waiting for us to start.

Chris and I have prepared three songs, mostly because they're all we know, but also because the hospital told us not to play much more, the patients would need their rest. We move to our makeshift stage, a couple of instruments gathered in a corner, and I stand before the chapel microphone. I cough out an introduction, something stupid that draws a few smiles and blinks. Then I turn back to Chris, and he nods the signal. We start to play.

We sound rough at first, filtered, the slow strain of Play-Doh through clenched fingers. Chris has brought drum brushes, not drumsticks that would drown out my guitar in this small space, and the scratches keep time with my voice, a voice that now sounds cracked as I gasp out the first few lines of our opening song. We've agreed on "Patience," my favorite Guns N' Roses ballad, followed by Pink Floyd's "Wish You Were Here"—Chris's pick, and one I've agreed on. But Chris has let me decide on the last song, and I've chosen one just for Mom—the Beatles' "Across the Universe." The chords aren't easy, and Chris and I have spent days mastering their progression. But Mom has always loved the song, and if I was ever to learn its notes, now was the time.

We falter through the first song, a warm-up at most since our audience doesn't react, and my voice is hoarse but not in the way that Axl Rose might have wanted. My face flushes as we proceed straight into our second song, but when I look up for the first time, I can see Mom and Dad off to the back. They're both smiling at me. The rest of the small crowd—maybe ten patients, and a few people who look like family members, plus three nurses and the ward director—they all look half-interested at best. But their faces suddenly fade into nothing. I know why I'm here. I have little more than a song left to get this done.

My voice rises, maybe not in volume, but in some degree of strength. Chris notices the change, his percussions grow in zeal, and by the second verse our instruments are belting out Pink Floyd, and I start to imagine what this noise might do. I picture sound waves floating from my fingers, my voice, Chris's hands. I picture them billowing from this room, down the hall, into Mom's room and inside her monitors and tubes. I picture them infiltrating her veins right here in this room, a surge like a quiet explosion through her brain, her brave heart, her small, pale hands.

And then we are to the last song, and I look up and she is smiling. She is smiling so large bright tears well at the corners of her eyes. Dad is smiling too, like he once did, before everything broke. And that is when maybe I know it has happened—that the world is just like the story said, that for once these notes and chords can inject life straight into our chests, just like the stick figure I drew, just like a ship setting sail toward the sky. I glance back at Chris long enough for him to look at me and grin, and for one perfect moment all is right, we are here, we are all alive in this room where sound and waves and molecules oscillate beneath the steady rhythm of these drums, my voice, our hearts all pounding as one.

And then it is over. Our last song peals a final cadence of notes, and for a second the room falls silent. Mom claps first—she claps so loud that she stands to support the movement of her hands, and Dad stands too, partly to clap, but also to watch her so she doesn't fall. I see Mr. Winchester to the left of them, and he's clapping and smiling too. Chris and I both take awkward bows, and we smile back at the audience. But our moment is over, leaves as quickly as it came, and the room is just a hospital room, the ward like any other on this earth.

I know what will come. I know that the patients will trickle back to their rooms, that Chris will leave with his dad, that when my dad and I pack the equipment back into the van and drive home, he will whisper over to me, his eyes still on the road, you know, Mike. You know she's not going to make it. And I know my mom will pull me aside in her room, once we've tucked her back into her bed and Dad has ventured off to use the men's room, and she'll look at me in a searching way and say, sweet, is that why? Oh, honey, it's just a story. Didn't you know?

But in my head—right now, while we're still standing here—it sounds better.

In my head, I am still singing, even as the energy leaves this room, even as the oncology ward becomes just what it was. In my head, I am still singing; I am playing guitar better than I ever could tonight, maybe I'm even playing the violin, a meaningless difference now.

In my head, she is not in bed hooked up to IVs, she is not so weak she can barely stand, she is nowhere near this wasted floor. She is somewhere else, I don't know where, but she's with me, and she is safe. She is somewhere I can keep her, and we are taking flight, up, away from this place, so far up I can no longer see the ground.

TERRIBLE ANGELS

Sometimes they're there, sometimes not. Tonight they are, standing next to the television set, a distraction as Francie watches *Wheel of Fortune* with her dad, a bowl of popcorn between them on the couch—light butter only, to protect the ticker, he always says—and she knows he can't see them, he's oblivious, shouting vowels and consonants at the screen.

"*A*, you moron, just buy an *A*!" he yells, the couch cushions sinking beneath his weight as he leans forward. "Jesus Christ, Francie, am I the only one in the whole goddamn world who knows it's *aardvark*?"

He's not. She knows it too. But she's lost interest in Pat Sajak's clever jabs, the way his subtle goading provokes the contestants to buy more and more vowels. She's watching her grandparents instead, who have been standing by the television for over five minutes. They never speak when they appear, and sometimes it's just one of them, her grandfather or her grandmother, though tonight they've come together. They look just like she remembers, not aged to the way they'd look now, if they were still alive.

"Well, look at that, Francie. Mr. Bowtie Surprise finally solved the puzzle."

Francie forgets her grandparents for a moment, just long enough to cringe at her father's habit of assigning people arbitrary names, of labeling them according to clothing, or mannerisms, or the type of sandwich they eat for lunch.

"His name is Ron, Dad."

"Well, old Ron there is wearing a mighty big bowtie."

Her grandfather laughs, though no sound comes out. He's always liked her father, though she can see her grandmother scowl, roll her eyes. Her mother would have too, if she were still around. But she's not, and Francie wonders sometimes, when her grandparents appear in the back seat of her car, or next to her in line when she's picking up a pack of cigarettes at the 7-Eleven down the street, if the ghost of her mother might ever come as well, and if it did, whether her own ticking heart would burst and cease.

"How 'bout those SATs, sweet? Tell me again when you're taking those."

The game show has cut to commercial break, her father's attention on her now. He picks at the bowl of popcorn, stuffs a few puffed kernels in his mouth.

"Two weeks."

Her grandmother looks up when she says it, frowns.

"You ready? Nervous? Lying awake in anticipation?"

"None of the above. I haven't really thought about it yet."

It's the fall of her senior year and she's taking the SATs for the second time, later than most. She had signed up the spring before but failed to show, the test only three weeks after her mother died. She'd told her dad she was going, but picked up Marcus instead and they'd spent the day lying in a wheat field, smoking pot, identifying tricycles and snow globes in the clouds above.

"I'll drive you to the test myself." He grabs another handful of popcorn, smiles at her, pats her hand. "We can even do some flashcards, you know, verbs, nouns. Isosceles triangles. All that brainy shit."

Francie knows he'd have offered this before, that he's not just making empty promises, trying to be the dad he never was now that her mother is gone. He'd helped her study the first time around, though now she thinks maybe he'd been distracting himself too, a way to forget the world as it was.

The game show returns, her father sits forward again on the edge of the couch. Ron has advanced to the bonus round and stands before the five letters of the word WHEEL, ready to choose the hidden prize.

"Pull the *L*, Bowtie!" her father shouts, then lowers his voice. "The *L* is always the RV, Francie. The *L* is the one we want."

Francie tries to feign interest, tries to pour every ounce of her brain into which letter Ron chooses, to ignore her grandparents' presence. But as Ron pulls the second *E* and her father winces and mutters *Good job, Bowtie*, her grandfather lets go of her grandmother's hand and floats over to sit in the armchair beside Francie. She gasps a little, puts her hand over her mouth so her father won't see.

"I know, what a moron, right? He should've picked the goddamn *L*!"

Her father gets up to grab a beer, to return the now-empty popcorn bowl to the kitchen, to leave Francie on the couch to stare at her grandmother, at her grandfather, wondering why they are here.

———

In the afternoon quiet of the kitchen, as Francie sits reading her SAT prep guide, the sound of a car engine permeates the double-paned windows, roars up, settles in the driveway. Francie knows it isn't her father, knows he's working the second shift at the construction plant today and won't be back until well after dinner. When she gets up and looks out the front window, she isn't surprised to see Marcus's hunched figure, bulked in a hooded sweatshirt and too-large jeans, moving toward the door. He's smoking a cigarette and his face is lowered against the wind, his dark hair falling across his forehead.

Her grandparents haven't shown themselves today. Sometimes they go for days without turning up, just long enough for Francie to pretend this is some fluke of imagination, a rare incident she'll never have to explain. But when she opens the door and lets Marcus in, they are standing behind him on the doorstep. Her grandfather holds a jug of milk, her grandmother a bag of chocolate chip cookies. They both smile, great big smiles that make Francie's stomach plunge.

She shepherds Marcus inside, pulls him in so quickly that maybe, she thinks, her grandparents will stay outside. But as Marcus heads to the fridge to grab himself a Miller Lite without asking, Francie watches as her grandparents move through the door, milk, cookies, smiles all intact.

"This SAT shit again?"

Francie walks into the kitchen, finds Marcus leaning over her prep guide. He's already opened his beer, which sits on her book, as if it were a coaster.

"No more of that this afternoon." He slides over and sneaks his hands around her waist. She can see the guide over his shoulder, a circular watermark bleeding onto the chapter she's just begun, the one on geometry.

As she lies down on her bed and Marcus pulls off her shirt, Francie looks up to see her grandparents perched near the ceiling, elbows on their knees, hands no longer holding cookies or milk.

"Can you close the blinds?" she asks Marcus, and once he does the room swallows itself in darkness, so dark she can't see her grandmother or grandfather or Marcus's hands moving toward the zipper of her jeans.

Later, after Marcus has drunk three more of her dad's beers and finally gone home, Francie heats up a plate of leftover meatloaf and sits at the dinner table again. She is halfway to her first bite, fork suspended midair, when she stops, sets the fork down, mouth as open as her eyes. On top of her SAT guide, where the watermark had been two hours ago, sits a plate of three chocolate chip cookies, one glass of milk. And alongside this snack—tangible, not ghostly, she touches it to make sure—is a twig-and-twine grappling hook, the kind she once made in her grandparents' backyard.

In the car the next day, as Francie and her dad sit in traffic, she looks over at him and turns down the volume. They are on their way to dinner, someplace nice he's said, because he hasn't seen her since Sunday, because he's worked the night shift all week.

"Hey, remember those grappling hooks?"

"What grappling hooks?" He's half-singing along to Roy Orbison, an old tape he's kept in the car for as long as Francie can remember.

"Those hooks I used to make, at Grandma and Grandpa's."

"Those branch and string contraptions you used to build? The ones you thought you'd catch raccoons with?"

"Those are the ones."

"My God, Francie!" He laughs and looks over, his face like a kid's before a glowing birthday cake. "I haven't thought of those in years!"

"Did you keep any of them?"

"What? Oh no, France, I didn't keep any of them. But goddamnit, now I wish I had." His eyes settle back on the road, though his smile hasn't disappeared.

Francie hasn't thought of them in years either, even forgot she'd ever made them until one appeared and sat there like a question mark on her open book. Her grandfather taught her how to make them, held her hands beneath his as she tied the string tight and let the claw-shaped branches fly into the trees. Once it's secure you can climb, he'd said. You can perch up there and wait for raccoons.

She never had. The branches were too delicate, the trees too high.

"You know, you weren't a mean kid," her father says. "You talked a big talk, told your grandpa you were hunting. But we all knew you were just waiting to squeeze one of them, catch a fat raccoon and tuck it into bed with you. Like a big stuffed bear!"

Francie doesn't know why, but this is something she doesn't want to hear. The inside of the car has gone completely quiet, so quiet it hurts, and she reaches over and turns up Roy Orbison, to drown this all out, to blink everything back.

"What made you think of—oh, mother*fucker*!" Her dad slams the breaks, flips his middle finger at a white minivan cutting into his lane. "Go on! Go right ahead! The whole goddamn lane's just for you, asshole!"

Francie looks out the window, at the strip malls and banks along the road, relieved her grandparents aren't in the car, glad she doesn't have to watch her grandma roll her eyes again.

"Sorry, sugarbud." Her dad stares at the minivan's bumper. "Christ, what was I saying?"

Over dinner, when her father orders her a glass of red wine too, to *let loose!*, he says, before the big test next week, Francie feels him peek at her over his plastic menu.

"I noticed some of my beers were gone the other night. You been drinking to sustain your hard habit of study, or has that boy Marcus been by again?"

"He comes by sometimes. Big deal, Dad. I'm almost eighteen."

"Oh, right you are. A big adult!"

Francie rolls her eyes, sets her menu off to the side of the table.

"Look, France, you can do what you want. It's not you I'm worried about. I just think that boy's a goddamn loser."

Other girls would be annoyed by this, Francie knows. She imagines her friend Holiday hearing it from her own dad, envisions her flipping the table, storming out like a bad sitcom sketch. And though she thinks she could do the same—her dad would actually apologize if she did—she feels the will to do so deflate from her lungs. Her father is not her enemy. He is not her enemy, and he is right.

"You don't even know him."

"Oh, and you do? Ha!" He sips his wine, for emphasis, she thinks. "Look, sugarsnap, all I'm saying is you deserve better. That boy's nothing but a lump of mush."

Francie waits for her food, and for an indignation that never comes.

Later, after they've had dinner, after she's finished the math section on proofs and has moved on to the verbal chapters, she lies on her bed and looks up at the ceiling, at the place where her grandparents had been. Though she hates when her father is right, hates the haughty jest in his voice, she knows too that when she thinks of Marcus it is not with infatuation, not even with lust, but with the slow palpitation of an irregular heartbeat, a heart not even challenged by the strain of movement.

She hadn't known him before her mother died. But after the policeman came to their door, after the impact of collision shattered her mother through the windshield and her own life in a moment passed through some irreversible door, she woke up as if in a haze, sitting at her desk in homeroom after the funeral, had looked up sleepy-eyed and there he was.

When Francie's phone rings, she half expects to hear her grandfather's husky voice on the other end of the line.

"So you have to sleep over this weekend," Holiday says, her voice almost breathless. "Julie Sussman's having a party. Will said he'll kick Marcus's ass if he shows up."

Will is Holiday's boyfriend, a tall, lumbering fellow who never talks, and Francie has always been distracted looking at him, his forehead too large for his face.

"What?"

"Oh, come on, Francie. Like you haven't heard."

Francie narrows her eyes, focuses on the mobile of aluminum airplanes still hanging from her ceiling, airplanes her mother made when she was five.

"Marcus slept with Alicia Traver. He's been telling everyone you're too fucked up to date. You know, because of your mom and all."

Francie stares at the mobile. It's the last part that hurts, not the first.

"So you're sleeping over, right?" Holiday is indignant, her voice disclosing all of the rage Francie herself should feel, if she could reach deep into her chest and pull out a glowing ember. But when she thinks of Marcus, of his stooped shoulders and stringy hair, she thinks of only mush, her father's words, a pile of gray nothing that has smothered the burn to cinder.

"Sure. I'll sleep over."

As she hangs up the phone and crawls beneath her covers, she sees her grandparents peeking in her bedroom window, and a small pail of sidewalk chalk hanging from the airplane mobile, where minutes before there had been none.

On Saturday afternoon, after Francie has plowed through the chapter on analogies, she takes the pail out to her driveway and grinds the chalk into the pavement. She draws a hopscotch grid, the boxes big and angry, and skips through them like she once did in her grandparents' driveway, stomping her feet heavily against the asphalt.

"What're you doing there, bud?"

Her father stands on their front porch, a beer in one hand, a bag of cheese puffs in the other.

"Nice lunch, Dad."

"Well, it sure as hell beats hopscotch, Miss Skip to My Lou."

Francie picks up another piece of chalk, drags it hard along the pavement, her hair hiding the scowl on her face.

"Look, little britches, I'm just checking in. You seem down these days."

"Marcus cheated on me."

She doesn't know why she says this, since she's not sure it matters, or if it even qualifies as cheating. Marcus was never really her boyfriend to begin with. But she refuses to look at her dad, at the self-satisfied look that will color his face, and digs the chalk into the ground, expecting him to admonish her or make light of the situation somehow, or at least tell her that Mr. Lump-O-Mush was nothing but bad news anyway.

But *oh Francie* is all he says, his voice tinged with the filaments of sympathy, and when she looks up again he is standing right beside her, his eyes on the scribbles she's sketched into the asphalt.

"I'm sleeping at Holiday's tonight."

"All right."

Francie stands and drops the chalk. They both regard the hopscotch grid awkwardly. Her father sets his beer and cheese puffs in the grass. He begins hopping through the boxes, and Francie feels the gurgling urge of both laughter and tears welling impossibly within her. But before she allows either to erupt, she jumps through the boxes behind him, and they hop together without eye contact or words, without her grandfather or grandmother hovering over to watch.

But in the driver's seat that night, as she and Holiday head to the party, Francie looks up to switch lanes and spots her grandfather peeking at her from the backseat, his image just barely visible in the rearview mirror. The sight doesn't shock her; she anticipates his presence everywhere now, and she ignores him until they arrive at the party, until the doors slam and the car is locked tight.

"You ready for this?" Holiday asks, heels shaky, clicking against the walkway to the house. She's already had three beers, the reason Francie drove.

When they walk in, Will is already inside, holding a cup of beer and waiting near the door.

"Marcus is out back," he says, before they even take off their coats. "Where the fuck have you guys been?"

Francie stares at his face, at his hopelessly large forehead over the top of Holiday's thick hair as she stands on her toes to kiss him. Will puts his arm around Holiday, beer limp in his hand, and motions them both toward the back of the house. Francie feels her body go numb, her face fall blank, but she cannot stop herself from following them through the crowded living room, the beer boxes that litter the kitchen, on out to the backyard where Marcus stands smoking a cigarette.

It doesn't take long. Before Marcus turns around, Will hands Holiday his beer, slams his empty fist into Marcus's jaw. Francie watches the half-smoked cigarette fly from his mouth across the patio, landing somewhere in the grass, out in the dark. Will grabs Marcus by the elbows, holds him pinned and facing Francie, a small line of blood leaking through his two front teeth.

"Here it is, France." Will's breath steams from his mouth. "Your chance to get this fucker good, give him what he deserves."

Francie stares out at the grass, wonders where the cigarette went, whether it could smolder into flames and set the whole house ablaze.

"Come on, Francie, kick him in his fucking nuts!" Holiday yells, eyes swimming wildly between all of them, hands like claws around Will's beer.

Francie looks at Marcus's shoes, at the softness of his belly exposed by the angle of his elbows, and for a flashing moment she feels rage—not for love, but for the indecency of what he's done. But when she sees her grandfather hovering just behind Marcus, off in the dark grass, watching her from behind a set of patio furniture, she thinks of nothing but her mother, a strange memory at this moment, her mother testing the water for her bath once when she was four, making sure it wouldn't scald her, filling the tub with rubber whales and toy ducks, the kind that kicked through the water if wound just right.

"Let him go."

Will looks at her, body rigid, struggling against Marcus's strained arms. "What the fuck did you just say?"

"I said let go. You heard me."

Before Will can protest, before he and Holiday tell her how much Marcus deserves this, how they've waited three days to catch him here and make him pay, Will shoves Marcus onto the grass and Francie walks back inside.

"Hey, where are you going?" Holiday sounds annoyed, voice garbled by beer, and Francie wonders whether she will even remember this tomorrow, after Will has driven her home, after she's vomited the night across her bedroom carpet.

"Home."

They do not stop Francie as she walks back through the kitchen, the living room where Julie Sussman pulls a keg stand off her own couch, and out the front door into her car where, as she turns the key in the ignition, she sees a pogo stick in the rearview mirror, laid gently across the backseat.

Her father is not watching television when she walks in the front door, as she half expects him to be. She hears music wavering from the upstairs office, the muddled sound of Patsy Cline.

"Is that you, butterbean?" he yells down the stairs. "Early night?"

When she walks into the office, he's sitting in front of the computer playing solitaire. He's changed the card deck to the haunted house pattern, along with a three-card deal, though Francie prefers the beach.

"What's that you got there, a party favor?"

She doesn't know what he's talking about until she feels the pogo stick in her hand, resting at her side.

"Something like that." She thinks of the pogo sticks her grandparents kept in their garage, how she'd once spent a whole afternoon with her grandmother bouncing up and down their street until the sun sank behind the trees, until they went inside for pot roast and ice cream floats.

"Dad?"

"What is it, sweet pea?" His back is turned to her, his eyes on the screen.

"Can we watch a movie?"

He takes his hand off the mouse, looks at her, and for the first time she sees something sad in his face, something not unlike the way his entire body had collapsed once their guests left the house after the funeral, after he'd scraped the last of the deviled eggs and ranch dip into the waiting, open trash can.

"Sure, France. We can watch a movie."

He makes popcorn while she changes into her pajamas, and when she meets him downstairs in the living room, he's already settled on the couch, the title menu for *Mary Poppins* cued up on the screen.

"Mary Poppins?"

He peeks at her over the back of the couch. "You got a better idea?"

He hits the play button and grabs a handful of popcorn, and she sits down next to him on the couch, reaches for the popcorn too.

"Can you still take me to the test?"

"Sure, sugar beet."

She thinks of the pile of flashcards she's made, a series of analogies, vocabulary words.

"Can you help me tomorrow?"

He nods, grabs another handful of popcorn, his eyes on Mary Poppins sitting on a cloud, high above London.

"Next Saturday, if you want, we can get lunch after the test, maybe even a couple of blizzards from the Dairy

Queen. My God, look at Miss Umbrella float on down to town like that!"

Her grandparents do not appear again that night, but the next day, while she and her dad sit in the living room going over flashcards, a knock rattles the door and her grandparents are both suddenly there, sitting on the loveseat, holding hands and smiling.

"Who could that be on a Sunday?" Her dad looks out the peephole, then his body stiffens and he lowers his voice. "It's that goddamn mistake of a human being, France. You want to see him, or you want me to break some kneecaps?"

Francie ushers her father into the kitchen before she lets Marcus in, but can still hear her father grumbling *mush* to himself, just loud enough for her to hear through the closed kitchen door. She lets Marcus into the foyer, doesn't offer him a seat. Her grandparents are on the couch, and she doesn't want him to stay.

"I just came to say sorry." His hair hangs across his cheek, not long enough to hide his bruised lip, crusted teeth.

Francie says nothing, stands uneasily as her grandparents shift on the couch, both of their faces expectant and eager.

"I figure none of this really matters," Marcus continues, "and if you wanted, you could be my girlfriend. Like, for real."

Francie looks at him, her heart slowed to a dull murmur, nothing more. She glances over at her grandparents and they are laughing, with silent, wide-open mouths.

"So?" Marcus asks. "You want to?"

Francie feels her own laughter bubbling up, a laughter that could have been loud and free, like her grandparents' might have been, had their vocal cords produced sound. But she swallows the gurgle back, suppresses the urge so he will leave, her face passionless, indifferent to make him go.

"No," she says. "No, I don't."

Marcus looks up, his eyes cracked with hurt, a hurt that no longer penetrates, its shards small and useless at Francie's feet. He stands for a second, his mouth open as if to speak; then he seals his lips and turns, baggy jeans dragging on the carpet as he goes.

When Francie closes the door, hears her dad yell *That's my butterbean!* from the kitchen, she's too distracted to be annoyed, by the exhilaration of making Marcus leave, but also by the emptiness that suddenly bounces from the living room walls. Her grandparents are not on the couch. They've disappeared as quickly as they first came, without leaving any proof they might have been here, no cookies, no milk, no grappling hooks strewn across the couch.

"Dad?"

"You want a turkey sandwich for lunch?" The sound of his voice fills the room.

"Sure," Francie calls, then grabs her flashcards and takes them to her room.

Her grandparents are not there either, not in the windows, not on the ceiling; no pails of chalk, no pogo sticks along the floor. But as Francie sits on the edge of her bed, knowing this might be it, that she must grow accustomed once more to seeing their faces only in yellow-edged photographs, she leans back and her hands brush something rubbery, something plastic, something inflated.

She turns to find a pair of orange floaties, the water wings she once wore, though she knows these are not remnants from her grandparents' house, but from the baby pool that once graced her own backyard. They are the water wings her mother placed carefully on her arms, puffy rings encircling baby fat, protection even in two feet of water in case she ever slipped.

Francie does not know if these floaties will stay, or if they will disappear by the time she tucks herself into bed as the chalk, as the pogo stick and grappling hooks have all done. But she curls herself around them and hugs them to her chest, until she almost falls to sleep next to them, until her father at last calls her down for lunch. She leaves them upon her bedspread, their rubber tangible as memory, her mother's hands holding up her arms, and keeps them in her sight until the doorframe swallows them, until she passes from the room and lets them go.

A TASTE OF TEA

On the day my father told my mother he wanted a divorce, she went to the computer and ordered a pile of tea. He'd been seeing his dental hygienist for six months, something my parents didn't tell me, but which I heard anyway, listening to their terse discussion in the kitchen from the top of the stairwell. My mother called him a dirtbag but didn't sob or scream, and after my father stormed out of the house I peeked through the wooden banister and saw my mom down in the living room, sitting in front of the computer, staring blankly at a screen full of teas. I don't know how she found the website, or even why a company would offer a service like that. She didn't cry, just sat there punching credit card numbers into the keyboard, and three days later, as I was doing my geometry homework for summer school, I heard a shaking rumble outside and looked out the window to see a delivery dump truck backing across our lawn, unloading a giant mound of green tea in our backyard. The pile was the size of a safari anthill, and my mother was sitting next to it, laid back in a reclining lawn chair.

"What are you doing?" I asked, coming outside to see it.

She pulled her sunglasses down and looked at me. I could hear the dump truck down the street, roaring away.

"It's tea, Kevin. For me."

"But what's it doing here?"

"What *wasn't* it doing here, before?"

I stared at her. "Okay," I said. Then I walked back up to my room and sat at my desk, and watched her out the window, lying there next to the tea, her body sprawled across the lawn chair, her face turned toward the sun. The pile sat like a big dark Grimace next to her, and every once in a while she'd reach over and pat it firmly on the top, its dry leaves sticking to her fingers.

My dad was officially gone then, a quick departure to the apartment of the hygienist, whose name was Blanche. When my mom heard her name, she yelled, "What is this, *A Streetcar Named Desire*?" but that was all the anger I heard from her, and now my dad was supposed to return piecemeal, retrieve his things while Mom was at work, though I'd already seen his coat hangers and old flip-flops poking out of the trash cans at the end of our driveway.

I was fifteen, driver's permit in hand, and though one of my parents was supposed to be in the passenger seat each time I took the Buick out, this didn't seem like the time to ask either of them for permission. I called Blake instead, still watching Mom pat her tea pile out my bedroom window, and when he arrived on his bike a half-hour later, I grabbed my mother's car keys.

"We're going out," I yelled from the driveway. Dad had recently repaved it, black and tar sticky in the afternoon heat.

"You kids have fun."

I stood there a minute, but she didn't move or ask where we were going. A light wind blew small bits of tea across the yard.

"We'll be back later."

"Is that Blake with you?"

"Hello, Mrs. Gibbons," Blake called from the car, already in the passenger seat.

"How about Ms. Cornwall? My name's the better one anyway."

Blake looked at her out the window, but she just lay there, unmoving, her face completely blank.

"Tell your mom she needs to come over for a highball sometime."

Blake looked at the pile. "What about iced tea instead?"

I opened the driver-side door and turned the keys in the ignition, pulling out of the driveway before my mom had the chance to respond. Once we were safely down the street, Blake switched out her Michael Bolton cassette tape for the Black Sabbath he carried in his pocket.

"What the fuck was that?" Blake asked. He shoved Michael Bolton into the glove compartment.

"What the fuck was what?"

"That giant pile of shit in your yard. Looks like your mom's gone loony."

I ignored Blake, reached over and turned the volume dial skyward.

"Where are we going?"

"Shakey's?"

Blake always suggested Shakey's, the ice cream stand that wasn't two miles down the road. We could have easily biked there, like we'd done all freshman year, but now that I had Mom's Buick, Blake thought driving was more adult. He also thought it would impress Callie Malone, a sophomore who scooped ice cream, though I was the one driving and Blake wouldn't be sixteen until May.

After we pulled into the parking lot, and after Blake made me roll past the ordering station with our windows down, *We Sold Our Soul for Rock n' Roll* blasting, Blake ordered a strawberry shake and that's when I noticed Helen Toll sitting at one of the outdoor benches with some other girls from our class. She was a redhead, freckles splashed across the bridge of her small nose, and she'd been my lab partner in freshman biology. She always smelled like an orange grove, which was heavenly back in January when the snow seemed literally stacked against the classroom windows, but I'd never found the nerve to really talk to her outside of class, just looking over her shoulder during exams instead.

"Looks like your lady's here." Blake sucked on his straw.

"So's yours." I glanced back at Callie at the ordering station, in her bright yellow Shakey's hat. She couldn't have looked more bored.

"Make your move, man." Blake sat down at one of the picnic tables, the condensation from his milkshake creating a darkened ring on the wood. "Girls like that seem all bookish, but she's probably got a pair of handcuffs under her mattress."

I looked over at Helen, thought of her spinning handcuffs in a red bikini. "She's not like that."

"How would you know?" Blake swirled the straw inside his cup, loosening clumps of ice cream. "I bet that girl sucks dick like nobody's business."

Heat rose beneath my skin, burned into my cheeks. "Why do you say shit like that?"

"Why not?" Blake smiled around his straw.

"Because it's jackass, that's why not."

Blake sucked up the last of his milkshake and crushed the cup in his palm. "You need a good fuck, Gibbons. No more of this eyelash-batting bullshit. You've got to take the bull by the horns and just fucking do it."

Since junior high, I'd only kissed two girls—Marcie Johnson in seventh grade, on the cheek because her breath smelled like potato chips, and Jenny Alfonso during a game of spin the bottle, the summer before freshman year. Her tongue tasted like red licorice. Blake'd had sex once, back in March, with a girl from St. Mary's. He thought he knew.

I looked over at Helen again. She was laughing at something one of her friends said, her head back and her eyes rolled up, red hair floating against her striped tank top.

"I should get back. I need to finish my geometry homework before tomorrow."

Blake gave me a look. He'd already let me know he disapproved of summer school, that I didn't need to be taking classes when we could be out driving around, talking to girls, smoking pot in abandoned parking lots.

When we pulled up to the house, my dad's car was in the driveway. It looked like it always did—a tan Honda with leather interior—except the headlights were smashed; the words I FUCK OTHER WOMEN were soaped into the back window, and VIOLENCE? was etched in large angry scrawl across the windshield. My mom was lying exactly where she'd been when I left, along the side of the house next to her pile of tea.

Blake hopped onto his bike, and I couldn't tell whether he was laughing or coughing as he sped away. I walked over to the lawn chair and stared at my mother.

"What the hell is this?"

She didn't answer, and I thought she might be sleeping beneath her sunglasses. But then she patted the other lawn chair, the empty one next to hers, and motioned for me to sit down. "I thought maybe your father'd be gone by the time you got back."

"So what, that makes it okay?"

She lifted her sunglasses and peered over at me. "There are things you don't understand, sweetheart."

I hated the *when you're older* card that teachers and other parents always pulled. Now my mom was pulling it too.

"There's a lot of violence in this world," she said, and it sounded so vague and weird that I thought maybe Blake was right, maybe she had gone crazy. But then she looked over at me, and I saw a defined sadness in her face. "Love isn't much more than a fencing match, Kevin." She reached over to her pile of tea, touched it again. "It's just a matter of who stabs who first."

I thought of Helen, of her and me lancing each other with swords, looked over at Dad's car again. "And that's your way of stabbing back? Is that what you're telling me?"

"Oh, honey. Maybe not. I hope it's something you'll never have to understand."

Later she would explain it—the conversations she'd had with my dad throughout their marriage, how livid and self-righteous he'd been about fairness, and treating people right, and how violence was at the root of all things, how people exerted their power over each other. He'd been an ethics major in college, when they met, long before he'd gone to dental school and met the hygienist he'd eventually fuck and leave my mother for. She told me later that his fierce justice had drawn her in, and that the gravity of it still held her unmoving when she thought of it just right.

All I knew was how stupid it sounded to me.

"I'm sure the neighbors are looking," I said. "And not just at the car. At this goddamn tea."

She lay back in her chair, flipped her sunglasses down.

"Let them look," she said.

That's when my father came storming from the house, clothes trailing on hangers behind him, a coffeemaker tucked under his right arm. He dropped the clothes and set the coffeemaker on the hood, and rubbed his palms across the windshield, looking up and down the street all the while. And then he walked over and screamed at my mother in her lawn chair, while she sat placidly next to her tea, and I crept unnoticed into the house and closed the door on all the noise.

The tea pile dwindled over the course of the week, laid waste in mysterious ways, since my mother was a small woman and couldn't have drunk that much by herself. She set out two pitchers of sun tea, plastic wrap stretched across the tops to deter flies and yellow jackets, but I never really saw her drink any of it, not from the window of my room anyway. By Thursday, the pile was gone. I thought that was it, that maybe she'd grown tired of sitting in her lawn chair after work, lying in the sun and keeping watch over the heap. But that Friday, while I was in the kitchen heating up a frozen waffle before class, I heard a dump truck roll up the street and looked out the front window in time to see another tea pile dropping into our yard, this time golden in color.

"Chamomile," my mom said, when I called her at work. "It's calming."

I looked out the window, watched the dump truck thunder away.

"The neighbors are watching," I said, even though no one was around.

"I'll be home after five today."

"Try not to destroy any of Dad's property on your way home." Besides the car, she'd obliterated Dad's old matchbook collection over the weekend by lighting them all on fire in the backyard while I was at the library studying.

When I came home from class that afternoon, the phone was ringing. I expected my mother, calling with special instructions about the tea, maybe asking that I stand guard all afternoon so ants wouldn't carry it away, leaf by small leaf. But when I picked up, it was Blake.

"Get your swim trunks on," he said. "We're going to the pool."

According to Blake, he'd been biking past the Montgomery Park pool and had seen a group of girls through the chain-link fence there, a group that included Callie Malone and Helen Toll.

"But they're not even friends."

"Au contraire." Blake's voice sounded muffled, like he was eating a donut. "They're both on the JV soccer team."

I sat back on the living room couch. I hadn't thought of Helen in days, had maybe even relinquished my crush, at least until September. I pictured the Montgomery pool, Helen lying back on a striped towel, the sun reflecting off the glossy skin of her bare abdomen and legs.

A half hour later, Blake was in the passenger seat of the Buick and I was driving the two of us to the pool, towels strewn across the backseat, sunglasses and flip-flops on, swim trunks catching in the breeze that flowed through the open car windows. Blake threw Mom's Michael Bolton in the glove compartment again, this time for Van Halen. I thought of her arriving home soon and sitting outside with her absurd pile of chamomile, her feet propped up on the heap, my father nowhere in sight. I crushed the gas pedal down.

At the pool, Blake paid admission for both of us, since I'd driven and he was in a good mood. It took me less than ten seconds to find Helen—her red hair was a bright torch in the afternoon sun, and she was standing in the shallow end of the pool, her hands held lightly above the surface like she was getting used to the water. Blake stared at Callie across the pool, stretched out on her towel, looking weird without her Shakey's hat.

"I'm going to go talk to her." Blake looked at me, then back at Helen in the water, shrieking a little each time a ripple hit her bare belly. "Now's your chance, man. Don't fuck it up."

I stood there for a second, watching Helen gradually immerse herself in the water until her red hair disappeared beneath the surface. I dropped my towel and t-shirt on a pool chair and sat down at the edge of the shallow end.

"Hey," I said.

Helen didn't look over, and something deflated inside my chest. It was like raising my hand in class and the teacher never seeing me, though the rest of the class had. I considered getting out, telling Blake I was going home. But just as I moved to push myself up from the edge, Helen said my name.

"Kevin!" When I turned around, she was smiling at me. "I didn't know you came here much." She said it like she came to the Montgomery pool every summer, like she knew I wasn't a regular. I mumbled something about my geometry class, that I needed the break. She splashed the water with her left hand.

"Why don't you come on in?" She squinted up at me. "It's a little cold, but you get used to it real fast."

I looked across the pool at Blake. He was sitting on Callie's towel now, leaning in like he might put his arm around her.

Since it was still mid-June, the water was shockingly cold, but Helen splashed me and laughed until I ducked my head underwater, and then it wasn't so bad at all. The sun warmed the back of my neck, and I relaxed into the water so I didn't have to think about how I was finally talking to her.

We floated along the edge of the pool together, and every once in a while she'd grab the side and kick her legs out, or slide her head under the water. She told me about her summer, that she was taking a PSAT course, that she'd gotten a job at the bakery on Northanger Street by the school, to make some money between soccer practices. I listened to her and tried not to think about her body just below the surface, a cascade of golden skin only inches away.

Helen was telling me her fall class schedule, excited that we had English during the same period, when the lifeguard blew his whistle and announced adult swim. I looked at Helen awkwardly, not knowing if we were old enough to stay in the pool.

"I could use a soda." She smiled. "You want to come sit with me?"

We grabbed our towels and moved to the concession stand. Helen stood in line while I found a table near the edge of the pool's chain-link perimeter, away from screaming children and tired parents. I looked over toward Callie's towel again and noticed it was gone. Panic gurgled in my belly, that maybe Blake had left me there. And that's when I realized it—that he'd taken her somewhere. Maybe the woods out back, maybe a deserted shower in the locker room. Wherever they'd gone, they wouldn't be back any time soon.

Helen walked up with a large soda in a Styrofoam cup.

"Sprite," she said. "You want a sip?"

"It's actually kind of hot out here." I pushed back my chair. "You want to go sit in my car? I can turn on the air."

Helen squinted down at me and said nothing.

"I guess," she finally said.

In the Buick, I turned down the Van Halen and we sat silently while Helen sipped her soda. Her swimsuit was still wet, staining the seat cover with dark damp. Blake would be angry when I took him home later, but I didn't care. Helen told me she was taking trigonometry in the fall, and that she might join the dance team, since it wouldn't interfere with soccer. She was talking about the same things she had in the pool, but her voice was different, like our conversation couldn't sustain itself in the new air of the car. Her hair was still wet, and as she spoke, a bead of pool water slid down her neck toward her swimsuit, crossing peach skin puckered with cold.

She was still talking when I asked if I could kiss her. She stopped and looked over at me.

I stared down at my hands. I could hear her breathing, the rise and fall of her exposed, perfect chest. And before she could say anything more, before she could maybe say no, I leaned across the front seat and kissed her hard across the mouth.

She kissed me back. I was sure of it.

With my mouth against hers, I thought of Blake, laying Callie down across some leafy forest floor, or pressing her against a mildewed shower wall. I pulled Helen toward me, one hand behind her neck. With the other, I fumbled my way up her towel and past her exposed belly until I found her breast. Beneath my hand was a grapefruit. Tangerine. A lemon, at best.

I fumbled harder, my tongue in her mouth, until she pushed me away, her soda spilling across the Buick floor. She stared down at the Styrofoam cup, the straw and lid scattered over the floor mat, and pulled her bikini top up so her breast was no longer exposed.

I wiped my mouth and leaned back in the driver seat, not knowing what to say to her. We sat there for a moment, and then she pushed open the passenger door and walked away. I didn't follow her, or even watch to see if she returned to the pool, or if she just went home. All I could hear was the muted sound of Van Halen and the slow fizz of Helen's spilled soda, pooling now in the corner of the floor.

I thought about Blake. He'd find a way home. I shifted the car into drive and pulled out of the parking lot.

I knew my mother would just be getting home, and I didn't want to see her. So I drove around, up and down Northanger Street, past the high school, and then to the playground of my elementary school, where I sat on a swing, waiting for the light of the sky to tilt away from me, toward dark.

When I finally pulled into the driveway, sometime after sunset, my mom was sitting outside next to her new pile of tea, like I figured she would be. She was lying back in the lawn chair and staring up at the new summer sky, twilight marbled in pink and orange across the horizon beyond the trees. She didn't even have to pat the lawn chair next to her.

"Mom," I said, sitting down beside her. I didn't know where to go from there.

"What is it, sweetheart."

"Mom, I think I did something wrong."

She didn't look over at me. "Oh, it's all right, Kevin. I haven't been easy on you either, these days."

"No. I mean, I think I hurt someone."

She didn't respond right away, and I thought maybe she was angry, until she said, "Fencing match?"

"I think I stabbed first."

She didn't say anything back, but she reached over and patted my hand. It was the first time I could remember her touching me since I'd started high school. Her hand felt like an afghan.

We sat there awhile longer, neither of us speaking.

"Is Dad ever coming back?" I finally asked.

"Oh, I don't know, Kevin. Probably not. But you'll still see him."

I looked over at the tea, the giant mound of it like a small home.

"Why tea, Mom? I mean, really?"

She didn't say anything, and I thought her hand still patting mine was all the response I'd ever get. But then she looked over at me, and there was that sadness again, the kind she hid like a diary.

"Because I can." She sighed. "Because it's mine."

I thought of Helen then, what was hers, what was never mine. The tea sat like a ghost between my mother and me, silent, almost floating. A light breeze blew past, scattering a few leaves, pulling the scent of dandelion and apples through the yard. I reached over and touched it and the leaves stuck to my fingers.

"You should try it," my mother said. "It's pretty good. It calms."

I touched a tea leaf to my tongue, expecting the same sugared scent. But there was no calm, no sweetness. There was only the sourness of the leaves, a taste too bitter to take.

EVERYTHING THAT WAS OURS

When the World's Fair came to Queens, we watched the flags slowly rise. We watched trucks haul in the Sinclair dinosaurs, the Pepsi pavilion, the Magic Skyway that would move us through the past to comprehend the future. We watched the steady construction of the Unisphere, twelve stories high, a stainless-steel globe tilted on its axis, a testament to the peace through understanding that the fair promised. We watched Flushing Meadows Park become another world entirely, from the other side of the Long Island Expressway where we all worked then, from the panoramic windows of Albertson's Ladies' Shoes.

Stan pressed his face to the glass between customers, watched the exhibition emerge and swore that these were the promises LBJ would break, now that Kennedy had left us all behind. He shook his head and turned away, while Breslin stayed and stared off toward the park, watched the signs roll up for the new Ford Mustang the fair would introduce, a car we knew he had the money to afford. Jim watched the General Motors ride materialize, a glide through the future that maybe reminded him of his dad, who worked for GM, whose blackened nails and oil-smudged fingerprints told a different story, a future apart from undersea vacations and desert irrigation. And me, I hung back and worked, fit sandals to high arches, slipped shoehorns beneath heels.

Stan was the one who got us jobs. We'd all met in college algebra, some core requirement at Nassau Community College where we sat in the back of the classroom and shared what minimal notes we took on polynomials, binaries. Stan's dad owned the shoe store in Queens, and we all needed the money. I was the one who took the job first—working mornings before class, then some Saturdays and Sundays—and then Jim signed on, then finally Breslin, for nothing better to do. Breslin's parents paid his tuition. We all knew that. He also had a Ford Falcon, and once Stan's dad hired him we all stopped taking the Long Island Rail Road and piled into the Falcon instead, on the days we could coordinate our shifts right, which was most of them.

Jim had been my best friend in high school, the only person I knew at Nassau when we enrolled, which was maybe strange for Levittown High being so close to the college, but then again, a million people lived on Long Island. We went to school, we worked. We fit women with shoes. Stan peeked up ladies' skirts when his dad wasn't looking. Breslin did the same, carried a magnifying glass in his back pocket for just that purpose, no matter how indiscreet he looked tilting the lens while women hovered above. Me, I once sold a pair of purple suede pumps to Peggy Lee.

We'd dicked around for two years. We'd smoked, we'd huffed, we'd bashed the mailboxes of every neighborhood we knew, until all of Long Island was only broken splinters of wood, a scatter of lost letters. We would graduate in May, less than a month away, over the staggering precipice of what, none of us knew, though for me it would be far, someplace so far away my mother's dull gaze wouldn't follow me—the plains of the Midwest, or maybe the other side of the Atlantic entirely.

It wasn't that I disappointed her. I would have traded my life for that, for the way Stan and Jim complained about their parents, their nagging questions about jobs and college. My mother no longer looked at me—only me, the me I was before we lost what we did. I saw it in her face, in the way her eyes shifted down, or to the side, or just past me when I spoke: that for her my shape carried a double, my presence would always imply an absence, the same eyes and hands and mouth and voice, the hint of Anthony in every movement and word.

My brother, Anthony, who gave me his trunk of baseball cards when he moved on to poker, who taught Jim and me to crack a bat against leather so we both made the varsity team before our junior year. Anthony, who slept in my room for two weeks when our father died, back when the shadows on my walls made monsters and I still sometimes wet the bed. Anthony, who came home from college upstate last Christmas, who slammed his car into a tree when it slipped on black ice, who left every one of us irrevocably behind.

My mother, she meant well. She cooked the roast chicken I loved and hugged me each time I left the house, the caked residue of her lipstick imprinted on my cheek, the ghosts of her fingers leaving hollows in my shirts, following me across Queens. But we watched the fair emerge through the palpable lack the holidays brought, through the embittered winds across the Long Island peninsula in January, and through the slow melt to spring, a thaw that left puddles in grandstands and pavilions.

Stan watched with disdain, his head in perpetual quake, his eyes cast down like fire to burn it all away. And though I worked through the slow build, ignored its formation like a city beyond the windows for the curve of women's heels, I considered it anyway, what potential we were promised, a future no Skyway could comprehend.

On the Wednesday in April when the fair opened its gates, Grandpa met me at Hartley's Diner, which he did sometimes on my lunch breaks from Albertson's.

"Did you know most heart attacks happen on Mondays?" he said, fork suspended above a plate of beef chili. "Mondays I eat my vegetables mostly, but life's short, Mike. You better eat every goddamn thing you want."

I sipped my coffee, nodded down into the black. He'd had heart problems since his fifties, but who were we to tell him what he could and couldn't eat.

"How's your mom, son? Still doing all right?" He speared his chili again, a dish that seemed better eaten with a spoon, but there again I couldn't tell him a better way to do all the things he'd done for years.

"Fine. Her job's going well."

My mother worked as a seamstress for a tailoring shop she'd opened herself, not long after my dad died. All of this Grandpa already knew. Sometimes he checked on her still, in the roundabout ways he knew how.

"And yours? You kids behaving yourselves around all those ladies?"

Though my mother had surely told him at some point to keep an eye out for me, in a way a father no longer could, Grandpa never asked about my future. He only asked about

Albertson's, stopping his questions at the bounds of what existed, not what might be.

"We've been watching that fair go up, out there across the expressway."

Grandpa's eyes widened. "Oh, yes. The grandest fair of all! Your mother wasn't much younger than you when the first one rolled around."

My mother had told me all about the 1939 World's Fair over dinners the past few weeks, as if remembering made her young again. She mentioned the planetarium, the color photography and air conditioning, the Westinghouse Time Capsule whose copy of *Life Magazine* had likely disintegrated to dust. The lines near her eyes softened, those memories smoothed them out, but then she'd look at me and they'd harden again, as though I'd lurched her back to a relentless march of moments that bore her away from the past.

"They rolled out the new Mustang at the fair." I knew Grandpa loved cars.

"Jesus, boy. News like that will give a man a heart attack." He grinned and leaned in like we were conspiring. "What do you say we skip over there, just check it out? Come on. You've got time."

I looked at my watch. A half-hour left of lunch, though even if I made it back late, Stan's dad never cared. He always told us he chose selling shoes over stock brokering so he could maintain his hair color through middle age without the wiry tinges of gray.

On our walk to the fair, Grandpa told me his weekly trip to the store had ended in disaster earlier that morning when he made it through three aisles of food before realizing that he'd accidentally taken someone else's cart back in the produce section.

"It was the peas I noticed." He shook his head. "Who buys fresh peas? From there I saw the sweet pickles, the walnuts, all things I'd never eat. The walnut skins, they stick to my teeth. I left the cart there, walked right out of the store."

I nodded and kept walking. I never knew what to say when Grandpa told me his weird stories. The week before, he'd caught his neighbor sunbathing in the nude and had thrown a towel out his window, told her to cover up before any kids saw.

We approached the fair's gates and moseyed inside. Crowds were still minimal—more people would surely flood the pavilions after work—and we moved inside with ease, walked past the flags of every nation and on toward the Unisphere, towering ahead. A middle-aged woman walked past us with a sheepdog, which bounded up to Grandpa and licked his hand before the woman pulled it away.

"Doesn't he look like a Dusty?" Grandpa stared after the dog. "It's a shame they can't tell us their own names."

We advanced toward the Ford exhibition, a large building with a line of people snaking out the front door. One Ford Mustang sat on a pillar outside, surrounded by a display of newly planted geraniums, a white convertible with red leather interior and chrome wheels.

"Now, that's a beauty of a vehicle." Grandpa whistled, stood back on his heels so his belly protruded. "A fine piece of metal indeed."

He was right. The car looked like an escape across the West, a wind-whipped joyride through the Badlands, some cross-country voyage to bear me away from Long Island.

"You know, your brother'd have loved to see this," Grandpa said, and then he stopped himself, looked down toward the tips of his shoes. I stared at the car. The sunlight glinted from every surface, puckered in diamond-shaped points that pierced my eyes.

"Your mother, Mikey." Nobody called me that but Grandpa. "I hope she's doing all right."

I told him I needed to get back, that Stan's dad would be waiting for me and we had sneaker orders to fill. Grandpa squinted and looked away, and I couldn't tell if the light hurt his eyes too, or if the car simply radiated something else for him, some shining sun he could have sat beneath all afternoon.

After work, and after Breslin took us all to the Burger Barn for shakes and fries, we drove past the fair on our way to the expressway, watched people milling like bees in a hive, the wind blowing past the windows as we accelerated up the merge lane.

"What a bunch of fucking morons." Stan flicked a cigarette out the passenger side and rolled up the window. "Like a fair will make a goddamn bit of difference."

Breslin laughed. "LBJ sends us all to Vietnam, slowly and steadily, but a brand-new Mustang is going to change everything, sure."

Jim rolled his eyes in the backseat, kicked the back of Breslin's chair. "Yeah, and you'll surely be the first to go. With Mommy and Daddy paying tuition, you can send us postcards from NYU, you jackass."

"From Harvard, Jim." Breslin grinned into the rearview mirror. "And food instead of postcards. Gold Mine Gum might be hard to find in the jungle."

At home, my mother had already gone to bed. A roast chicken sat on the kitchen counter with a note that the oven was still half-warm, I could heat it up if I wanted. I slid the chicken into the fridge and headed upstairs.

In my bedroom, I unbuttoned my Albertson's shirt and removed the undershirt beneath, one of a dozen white tees I'd gotten from Anthony when he outgrew them and then again when my mother finally cleaned out his closet. I'd hated hand-me-downs before, had yelled at my mom that I deserved new clothes too. Now, I'd wear them until holes poked through the sleeves, until no more hand-me-downs were left.

On top of my dresser sat a framed photo of Anthony, a gift my mother had placed in my room without words sometime after the funeral, as though it had appeared on its own. The photo had been taken at our last Fourth of July celebration together, after Anthony's high school graduation and just before he left for Albany. We'd lit a bonfire in the backyard like we always did, and there were hamburgers and hot dogs and Black Cats and cherry bombs. In the photo Anthony held a Roman candle out toward the sky, his other hand covering his eyes as he turned away from the blast. Grandpa smiled and looked on, out of focus in the background, which meant my mother must have taken the picture. She'd snapped it just as the candle burst open, a flash of sparks and light burning hot into the night.

I lay in bed and watched the ceiling, the puckered ridges of flecked paint. Though Grandpa never asked about the future, I thought about it anyway, how far away I could go, and where and what for. I hadn't applied to college, at least not back in the fall when I should have. My mother said SUNY would take me, in the moments we ever talked about the future, when she pushed her dinner around her plate and mentioned the possibility of rolling deadlines.

Breslin would go to college—his parents would see to that. We joked about the war, as uncertain as everyone else whether it was inevitable or not, but if the war came, we all knew with certainty that Jim and I would go. Stan, he might just work forever with his dad, until his draft number either arrived or failed to show.

I wondered about the war sometimes, if maybe this was best—that if Anthony had to go, he may as well have gone here at home and not far away in some tropical forest we'd never be able to envision or understand. My mother watched the news; I caught her watching the troops boarding planes sometimes, waving out to the camera with their young faces, their skin the same as Anthony's. She must have thought it too: that if she were to lose him, at least she hadn't lost him in the way so many other mothers would, with a telegram or a note, and without the physical confirmation of a wake and a proper funeral, no tangible evidence to make us let go.

The fair grew as we worked through April, people ogling the IBM films and the Bell System rides, the great moments of Abraham Lincoln delivered through simulated speech. The Long Island Expressway flooded gradually with cars, so steadily that Breslin began rounding us up early, pulling into our driveways well before eight in the morning.

On smoke breaks, we stood on the rooftops of Albertson's, Breslin gazing off toward the fair with disdain and sometimes pulling out his magnifying glass to try and burn the tops of people's heads below. I watched the flags, the Unisphere, the Sinclair dinosaurs lined up like a prehistoric parade. For a focus on the future they seemed out of place, ancient, their primitive size eclipsed by machinery and engines, the same objects Sinclair fueled. My mother had read in the *Daily News* that kids under eight considered Dinoland the greatest exhibit at the fair, and from Albertson's I could see children staring up at the brontosaurus, its head surely obscured by the blinding afternoon sun. My mother hadn't mentioned the other news, that our troops were increasing overseas. By August, nearly one million were expected to have embarked in steady, silent progression.

Grandpa came over for dinner on the last Thursday in April, since our lunch that week conflicted with his monthly bridge club meeting. My mother made a pot roast, breaking her steady diet of chicken, and filled the pan with carrots and celery hoping Grandpa would eat them.

"Isn't it crazy that chairs don't have seatbelts?" Grandpa picked at a carrot, then speared his beef instead. "Sometimes I think, good God, the Earth spins and spins, we could fall right out of our seats."

My mother watched Grandpa push his carrots under a slice of bread. "I finished the last bridesmaid dress today for that wedding in May. Burgundy dresses. Who chooses wine colors for spring?"

I pulled another piece of bread from the basket and ate my pot roast. There was never anything to report about my own job, only pumps and heels and cigarette breaks, and sometimes Stan mouthing off about his dad, both at the store and in the car on the ride home.

After dinner we sat in front of the television, watching the six o'clock newscast with the rhubarb pie my mother had made. She pretended not to notice when Grandpa got up to use the bathroom and came back with another slice.

"Yep, it's about that season," Grandpa said when the news turned to schools preparing for graduation ceremonies. "We'll be attending Mikey's here in a couple of weeks."

"I've made myself a tweed skirt for the occasion." My mother shifted her glance toward me, I saw her from the corner of my eye. "What comes after graduation, we're still not sure."

"He'll figure it out." Grandpa set his empty plate on the coffee table and gave my mother a look. "Mikey's got a good head on his shoulders."

She turned away, took his plate into the kitchen.

Later, after Grandpa had gone home with half the pot roast and three pieces of pie, I came down from my room where I'd been studying for my last American history exam. Silence filled the house, Grandpa's chatter gone, and my mother sat at the kitchen table alone sorting through sewing patterns.

"I'm starting to think I stitched that last dress wrong." She dropped the patterns in her hands. "Things have been too busy. That bride won't be happy."

I sat down next to her. She'd already cleaned the entire kitchen, pots and silverware washed and dried.

She looked up at me. "What are you going to do?"

"Maybe study. Watch some television."

"No, I mean, you." She squeezed the bridge of her nose, shut her eyes. "You, Michael. What are you going to do?"

Her eyes opened, hollow and tired, dark circles shading their undersides. The question and her face and the imploring tone of her voice, all of it pierced a flash of anger through me. I pushed myself away from the table, stood up so I was looking down at her.

"Since when do you care?" My voice sliced the stillness in the room. "Now that I'm two weeks from graduating, my future matters?"

She looked like I'd struck her. Her eyes slid away, back down toward the table, and her voice grew even softer than before. "You've got options, Mike. You've got SUNY, or any other college you want to go to. The deadlines roll through August."

"I don't have any other college." I stared at her; she suddenly seemed so unaware. "I have the draft, Mom, and as

long as that's true, I may as well get far away from here, forget Albertson's and this hellhole of an island and at least live
my life until I'm shipped away to God knows where."

She didn't even look at me. She just sat there, the patterns
scattered beneath her hands. The air in the house thickened,
too heavy for my lungs, so I grabbed my coat from the foyer and slipped out the door toward Jim's house, leaving my
mother behind.

When I walked up to Jim's, Breslin's car was parked on the
street. I crossed the grass to the backyard, where a sliding-
glass door sidled up to Jim's basement room, and when I
knocked, Breslin pulled open the door.

"Well, look who it is." He held a trigonometry textbook
in his hands, a class he and Jim shared. "We're nearly done
studying for this bitch of a test." Jim's head peeked out from
the background and he waved, and Breslin motioned me inside and shut the door.

I watched the last half of *Bewitched* while they finished up,
took a Schlitz from the basement fridge. When they were finally done, Breslin pulled on his coat. I thought he was going
outside for a cigarette, but Jim was wearing a coat too, and I
knew he didn't smoke.

"Come on." Breslin flipped off the television before the
predictable conclusion of the episode, the reveal that Darrin
wasn't actually having an affair. "We're going for a ride."

Outside the air thrashed cold through the car's open
windows, but the change was welcome and I inhaled the
lack of stagnation, a shift from the fog that hovered above
the kitchen at home. We picked up Stan, who was waiting
at the end of his driveway like he knew we were coming,
and then we sailed onto the expressway where the night

air slicked a balm across the car, a space open enough to breathe.

"Where do you kids want to go?" Breslin shouted over the din of the radio, the rush of the highway.

We always went to the same places, every time we went out. The Burger Barn, the Rusty Nail. The Maple Leaf on Thursdays for cheap beer before the weekend brought crowds. I looked out across the highway, could see the far-off metallic flash of the Unisphere glinting from the heart of Flushing Meadows Park.

"Let's go to the fair."

Jim looked at me. "It's closed, Mike. Let's get a beer instead."

"Let's go anyway." I was adamant. "Who gives a fuck if it's closed."

Breslin watched me in the rearview mirror, his mouth spreading toward a grin, and Stan shrugged in the passenger seat and rolled up his window. Only Jim looked like he didn't want to, but he consented anyway with a slow nod of his head.

The fairgrounds were empty when we arrived, the crowds long gone, but two night porters paced the perimeter of the park as we drove up. Breslin circled around to the 7-Eleven on Radcliff instead, and we sat in the fair parking lot drinking PBRs until the porters finally left, sometime well after two. By then, I was drunk enough to scale a fence.

Stan made a step with his hands that I climbed onto, hoisting myself up toward the railing until I flopped over the edge. Breslin followed, pushing off Stan's shoulders as he stepped into his palms, and then Jim helped Stan across the fence, remaining on the other side.

"Aren't you coming over?" I stood eye to eye with Jim, chain links dividing our faces.

"How the fuck would I get across?" Jim squinted back toward the car. "I'll stay here, keep an eye out for cops."

I pinched his cheek through the fence and turned away toward the park.

The pavilions loomed like monsters in the night, deserted, their shadows hulking high over the park. Breslin ran down the main thoroughfare, the flags billowing like ghosts above him, while Stan stared at the posters for Johnson's Great Society, the ride that took audiences through the annals of American history and on toward progress, the great strides we would forge into the future. I walked past the Disney exhibits, the tours of worldwide waters and prehistoric caves, until I arrived at the Ford pavilion once more and stood in front of the Mustang like Grandpa and I had done.

The car had dulled in the dark, without the sunlight to illumine its interiors or polish its wheels. The red leather had turned almost black, the body's paint transformed from a blinding shaft of light to no more than a muted phantom.

Grandpa knew Anthony would have loved this car. He'd known that just as easily as he knew never to ask about my future, a future that maybe he anticipated would never come. I stared at the car, at its red interior gone black beneath the half moon. There were so many ways I wasn't Anthony. Anthony would have taken my mother to the fair, bought her funnel cake and popcorn, paid her way through the Magic Skyway and let the light fill her eyes again like it must have back in 1939, when the weight of what would end was nothing more than an impossibility and the future rolled out plush ahead like a smooth, unbroken highway.

Past the Mustang, the dinosaurs loomed in the distance. I noticed how close they were to the road where Jim stood, where Breslin's car sat waiting.

I yelled out to Breslin, who stopped sprinting down the thoroughfare. Stan was still staring at the Johnson posters, but when I stuck my fingers in my mouth and whistled, he looked up immediately. Within minutes, we were all standing in the center of Dinoland.

The triceratops, the brontosaurus, they all towered too tall above us to really be moved. But near the section of baby dinosaurs stood several bird-like creatures, two of which were small enough to dismantle.

"Jim," I shouted across the parking lot, where he stood with hunched shoulders, his fists shoved deep into his pockets. "Pull the car around."

"I don't think that's a good idea, Mike."

"Oh, don't be such a crybaby." Breslin launched his keys across the fence, which Jim fetched with reluctance from the gravel. "Pull the goddamn car around. I'll drive from there, like you never even did anything."

Jim stared at us for a moment then turned on his heels toward the car.

By the time the Falcon sat idling against the fence, we'd already unhinged a small pterodactyl from the ground and Stan had pulled some feathered reptile so hard that it separated, its feet staying bolted to the ground though the rest of it had come undone. Jim stood outside the car, looking away toward the expressway while Stan climbed back over the fence. We handed him the birds until they were both stowed in the Falcon's trunk, until both Breslin and I had scaled the fence, until we were back in the car, pulling hard out of the fairgrounds.

"I can't believe you guys did that," Jim said, his head resting against the back window as we accelerated onto the highway. Breslin laughed and Stan lit another cigarette, and I watched the moon disappear behind the expressway's concrete barriers until we were shooting down the left lane and the centerline reflectors held the only light for miles.

It was well after four when Breslin dropped us all off. By then, my beer buzz had faded to a dim fatigue, and when Breslin took me home, last, I slipped from the car knowing he would hide the birds well, the only one of us with his own place, his own garage.

"Hey," he yelled as I walked up the driveway. "That might be the stupidest thing we've ever done." I could tell he was still drunk.

I nodded and turned away toward the house, but when his car disappeared down the road, the pitch black felt like the heart of some forest or jungle, so much worse and more real than all the stupid things we could've ever done.

When I awoke in the morning, a dull ache crowding my temples, my mother had already left for work. But on the table, she'd left the *Daily News*, which, when I flipped through it over coffee, contained a small story in the local section, the headline blaring *TWO FAIR DINOS STOLEN; SINCLAIR PRETTY SORE*. I drooled a few drops of coffee, wiped them away so my mother wouldn't notice.

The car fell silent on the ride to work. Stan and I had seen the paper, and Breslin, he'd watched a brief news spot on the morning broadcast, the reporter announcing that the damages totaled twelve thousand dollars. Jim just stared out the window, his conscience apparently clear, though he shot me sidelong glares whenever we stopped at red lights.

On my smoke break that afternoon, I watched people line up outside pavilions, like they had every day since the fair opened. Crowds twisted through the thoroughfares, bunched heavily near snow cone stands and demonstrations, and even continued to wind through Dinoland, despite the missing birds. When Breslin climbed up onto the roof after me, I didn't even have to ask.

"I'll drop them in some field late tonight" was all he said, and I nodded and turned away, stubbed my cigarette out, and went inside.

When I came home that night, after hearing Stan's dad talk all day about the dinosaurs, and after watching the crowds move endlessly through the fair from Albertson's windows, a rush of people without end, I found my mother sitting in the living room, hunched over the coffee table while the six o'clock news blared on mute.

"Hi." I sat down next to her.

"Hi." She didn't look up.

I noticed then that she was locked in concentration, examining an assortment of old photos scattered across our coffee table. I leaned forward on the couch and recognized what at first looked like a bunch of boring shots—armchairs, dressers, a bedroom set of a full-sized mattress and night-stand—as a series of inventory photos my father had taken a few years before he died, photos meant to preserve our family belongings in case anything perished or burned.

There was my father's closet in one photo, all his ties and shoes and a stack of white undershirts I still remembered. There were my mother's perfumes, lined up along a vanity table, and the contents of my nursery, a wooden crib and a basket full of stuffed rabbits and bears. But the photos my mother focused on were the ones of Anthony's childhood bedroom, and I followed her gaze to everything there.

A nightstand, small enough to fit only one lamp. A book-shelf full of children's picture books and tiny figurines and airplane models. A rocking horse in the corner, a pile of board games—Anthony's favorite had been Candyland. An old alarm clock, a quilt fastened to the wall, a dresser topped with two stuffed bears. Their waving, still arms seized the intractable core of my chest, the way no hands or small palms would enclose them now, all that potential and the anticipation of what a child could bring, everything gone, every blinding white speck of the world that was ours.

"I can't," my mother said, just words without thoughts.

"You can't what?"

She turned to me, her eyes full. "I can't lose you, too."

I looked away, toward the silent television where I could see them, troops lining up before planes. A newscaster spoke in front of the soldiers, turning and pointing every so often, before the broadcast switched abruptly to the fair. Dinoland rose up behind a different reporter, and though I couldn't hear her, I knew she was describing the stolen birds. Beyond her stretched an obvious void, the space where the dinosaurs had been.

My mother gathered the photos into a pile, her hands sweeping across the coffee table, and my stomach rippled up inside me, a flicker of dizzy nausea. Maybe the beer still rolled through my body, or maybe something else, something I had no name for, a future too impossible to comprehend. I thought of Grandpa then, what he'd blathered about the Earth spinning and spinning, and how I'd ignored what was true, how senseless it was that our chairs had no seatbelts. My stomach flipped and bucked and I wished I was fastened to the couch, both my mother and me, with the world spinning as it was, as if the balance of gravity itself had shifted beyond progress or promise and our quick collapse had finally come, the air too heavy to hold us.

BY LIGHT WE KNEW OUR NAMES

Through summer, we waited.

We waited through June, through July, when the sun ripped a white fissure from tree line to sky, a sky that burned all day and all night, turning away from us for only moments, four hours, five, settled into its own sleep. The days were long then, stretched wide and full of light, but for us, full of only bruises. Full of slaps across sunburned cheeks when flowers weren't watered, when dishes sat and scummed. Full of cuts from broken bottles held against our throats until we gasped yes, take my money, just take it and go. Full of scratches from the exposed metal of pick-up flatbeds, latticing the backs of thighs, hands held across our mouths to catch and crush the word *no*. They were long days full of spilling light, so much light it shadowed every hurt.

We waited through split lips, through whistles from car windows, through bribes brokered at the movie theater, *free tickets for a hand job*. We waited through failed lifeguard applications, through mocking glances at our muscles, through gazes that moved from arms to breasts, through allowances paid to our brothers, the extra change flipped our way, *go buy yourself a Seventeen*. We waited until Wren came late to the bluffs, one night in August, carrying a six-pack in one hand, the other covering her mouth where blood spilled between her fingers. She set her beer hard on our picnic table, removed her hand, slapped a wet, red handprint against the wood and said, *Enough*.

The bluffs were where we met then, past dusk, the sun finally glutted of its own glare, when the men of Willow at last left us alone, crept into corner taverns or living room couches, the bluffs our hidden shade, wooded shelter from others who still prowled. Willow, north of Anchorage, abandoned by miners seeking gold, leaving lines of sons behind, only occasional daughters, only us. And in winter, left by tourists too, once the sun discarded all adventure after September dimmed each day. We met among tall pines, separate blood, divided by arms and hands and hearts and lungs that all held the same wounds—mine were Kestrel's and hers were Tee's, Wren's were mine. We met to drink, to smoke, to scream every word ignored until they ricocheted from the rocks, until Wren came late, smacked a bloodied palm against the table, until she said low and steady, we need a plan.

We would wait, she said, quiet through summer, and through the weakening glow of early autumn. We would wait until the equinox brought new lights, northern streaks against black, burning bands into the sky after the men crawled home, after they'd forgotten the shape of our hips, our breasts, long stretches of night that we could climb inside, a cloak, some shroud of darkness where, beneath the pale glow of atoms, we could see our own hands to practice. We would wait, so quiet they'd never notice us gone, until we could learn to fight, for self-defense, for release, until

Wren's father never knocked her teeth into her gums again for something as simple as not taking out the trash.

I am angry, she said, bloodstained palms curling into fists. I am so fucking angry.

But why wait? Tee took a beer, popped the tab. Why the fuck should we wait? Why not start now, for Christ's sake?

Because the nights are too short. Wren stared at her, eyes red. The nights are too short, and the light we need, it's not here. Flashlights are too obvious.

Tee climbed on top of the picnic table. I'm ready now. She held her skinny arms above her head, the left baring dark bruises where her boyfriend Brett had held her down. We all knew he played rough, though she denied it, said some girls liked being handcuffed, slapped around.

Wren stared over the bluffs, toward Willow's blinking lights.

You know damn well that's foolish. My dad knows we come here. Your little playmate does too.

Tee lowered her arms, stepped off the table. I looked away as she tugged her shirtsleeves down.

Every one of us, they know we're here, Wren said. Let the girls have their time. But winter, it's better. Nights that long, no one goes out. No flashlights, no headlights.

Just then, a blue Chevy crept past. Headlights dimmed, closer to road than bluff, but Kestrel recognized the car, we all did, her brother, his carload of derelicts. Kestrel wouldn't say but Tee had seen it, behind the bleachers after school, her brother pinning her back by the elbows, taking dollar bills from his friends after they'd slid a hand beneath her shirt.

Kestrel stared at the car, watched the taillights fade beyond the pines.

Wren wiped her mouth, a streak of red staining the cracks of her hands cut by talc and detergent, long hours worked at the car wash, the paychecks her father kept, no wife, no guard over Wren to tell him no.

We will wait, she said, just a matter of months now. And though her voice held a lilt of hope, the word *month*—not weeks, days, not even the beating pulse of seconds—rolled away from us, prostrate, as long and terrible as the dull drone of flatlines.

Wren lived across the street from me, ever since memory allowed either of us to know one another, and through the open windows of my bedroom I heard her screaming sometimes, through the fixed stillness of summer air when every window shuttered open to let in what stale breeze flowed, our town too far north for air conditioning. I heard her screaming at her father, his roaring voice consuming hers, a match of aggression that splintered through my windows while I tried to sleep, punctuated at times by the sound of broken glass, dishes thrown, the piercing thud of fists.

She had it worse than me, I knew—no monstrous fathers in my home after mothers finally left, no brothers selling me to their friends, and no boyfriends holding me beneath the weight of them, not even lovingly, no tender hands against skin. There was only me and my mother, what felt like the only home without a man in all of Willow, and yet beyond our four walls I knew the insults and catcalls and touches meant to harm, the intent for me sometimes so much worse than for Tee or Wren. Every man in town knew I had no father. *Bastard whore*, they sometimes shouted, snickered *bush child* from mocking huddles—knew I had no daddy to go home to, no one to tell on them. My mother stayed away, never diverted from her well-worn path between the chemical plant and home, never told me who my father was, never mentioned what couldn't matter now.

So when Wren's flashlight flickered in her room, drove a shotgun path across the street into my own bedroom window once September burned away, once Willow swallowed itself in dark just past the school's afternoon bell, and after her father, my mother finally fell asleep before blue-glowing television sets, inside sweat-stained sheets, I threw on my darkest sweatshirt, my blackest pants. I climbed down the tree beyond my window, the Morse tapping of Wren's flashlight illuminating my path, casting my shadow against the house. I waited by the curb, breath steaming in October midnight, and watched the sky slowly begin to glow, green streaks then blue, climbing up from the horizon like colors on acid test strips, shimmering ribbons of light that I watched without words until Wren appeared. Together we walked, straight down the center of the street, no one out, our clothes black enough to hold us against night while the auroras bloomed around us, wavering curtains of emerald, bright enough to illumine our way.

Wren carried old pillowcases stuffed heavy with grain sacks, with hay. At the bluffs, Tee and Kestrel already waited for us, Tee smoking a cigarette on the picnic table and Kestrel sitting unmoving beside her, watching the borealis blossom in bands beyond the rocks.

Tee turned our way, jumped off the picnic table, stubbed her cigarette against dew-frosted grass. As Wren held one old pillow against her chest, gripped tight between white-knuckled hands, Tee walked over steady and slammed her fist into the center. Wren stumbled back, coughed, hay dust bursting from the pillow like volcanic ash. Tee rubbed her bony hand, stepped back and looked out over the bluffs, and in the glow of the northern lights I saw her eyes shimmer wet.

Tee, I said, then stopped when she looked at me, the glow revealing a bruise down her cheekbone, black cast green in the swirling skylight.

Fuck off, Tee said. She walked back to Wren where she punched the pillowcase again and again, Wren holding the edges tight, footing staggered across the uneven rock until Tee finally had enough.

Tee pulled the pillow from Wren's hands, held it steady against her own chest while Wren bent low to catch her breath, palms against her knees. Tee knew, we all knew, that Wren's dad had taken her paycheck again, had locked her earnings inside a small safe, kept for booze, poker, women. When Wren's breathing slowed and steadied, she stood to full height and faced Tee, eyes hard. She punched the pillow once, slow at first, then quicker until Tee's body shook with each blow, like a Western, a riddling of bullets.

I looked at Kestrel, who stood there by the picnic table, shoulders hunched, curled in on herself to protect what was hers, constantly taken. I grabbed the other pillow, resting heavy on the picnic table, and stood before Kestrel with it held against my breastbone, arms steeled and ready for the first tremulous blow. Kestrel raised her eyes to mine, and behind her the auroras wavered like brushstrokes, alighting glints of her hair and casting her face in indelible sorrow. Her eyes moved down to the pillow and fixed there, seeing what I imagined was more than thread counts, more than cotton. Then she punched, both hands clenched rigid—she punched so hard I felt what force was in her move through me, a kinetic quake, all the light she held inside her, some separate sun no one saw, eclipsed.

———

We'd learned all our lives what the auroras meant. In grade school, each year, the terms grew more technical, from atoms to photons to geomagnetic storm to solar wind, a flow of ions shot from the sun, colliding with the earth's magnetic fields. We learned the auroras' shades, their seasons, their steady growth past the equinox. We learned so much we traded wonder for routine, dozed, favored sleep over splendor, ignored beauty burst and blooming overhead, haloing our town. We loved and hated Willow then, how ignorance made us safe inside moonlight, unsafe beneath sun.

The days grew shorter, nights longer. And yet the days still felt stretched, even without light, all the hollers and whistles and barks filling the dark spaces the sun left behind, all our walks home, every walk to work. At the car wash, before her dad even made it to her paychecks, Wren suffered catcalls, her hands sliding sponges across hoods while boys shouted from backseat windows, *You can wash my hood anytime*, mocked and high-fived, tried to tuck meager tips into the waistband of her jeans. Kestrel avoided the bleachers after school, tried the shortcut through woods, and was cornered in the library bathroom instead, during study hall, locked in by Todd Marcus, her brother's best friend. He pinned her to the wall, slithered a hand down her pants. Threw five dollars against the tiled floor once he'd had enough.

And me, I took back roads too, through woods and past the river, twice the length home but worth the peace of tall pines and blackbird songs, after Jim Henshaw pulled up along the sidewalk, exposed himself from the car, said, *Who's gonna believe you, no daddy around?* He worked at the chemical plant with my mother, seemed nice enough when he'd given her rides home, waved from the driveway. When he pulled up beside me, I thought he'd slowed to offer me the same.

Thought a cougar caught my girl, my mom said, when I came home an hour late, pine needles piercing my jacket, back roads mired in bramble. She stood in the kitchen stirring soup in a pot. I ached to tell her how close to right she was.

Where you been, Teal? she asked, and when I didn't respond, she looked up. The smoke from the pot curled into her hair. What, big cat got your tongue? She laughed, and though I wanted to, I couldn't tell her. I couldn't tell her that despite the four walls she'd built around us, despite every warmth and meal and tenderness she'd laid before me, something had seeped through, water stains through walls.

I sat beside her, held the tongue that soup scalded, rolled the burn around my mouth while the television blared from the living room.

That night, Wren brought a bat. When I met her in the street, the lights illumined what she held in her hands, its mottled wood cast in pockmarked jade. Her eyes burned hard, phosphorescent beneath the charged sky.

My dad takes my paychecks, I take his bat.

I nodded and we walked. There was nothing left to say.

Kestrel sat alone when we arrived, perched on the picnic table, hands clutching her middle. She glanced at us, said Tee hadn't showed, then her eyes moved to the bat in Wren's hands, at rest but ready. Kestrel grabbed it, I'd never seen her move so fast, and she slammed it against a maple tree, bark splintering from root, chips bursting, revealing sap. She held the bat trembling inside her unsteady hands, then pulled back and smashed the trunk high, low, perpendicular to bark lines, sometimes parallel. She smashed and smashed, wood against wood, but the bat never cracked, never broke, until she paused, lungs steaming. Wren approached her then, from behind, enclosed Kestrel's hands inside her own, guided the bat. Even swings, steady. Practice, Wren told her, and Kestrel calmed. I watched the breath leak out of her, watched her arms move stable beneath guiding hands until her swing grew even, until Wren moved away, stood next to me again.

It isn't enough, she whispered near my ear, both of us watching Kestrel. It isn't enough to just be angry, to vent our wrongs. We need to be calculated, prepared.

As the northern lights flared above us, I looked at her and thought release, practice, slow build of muscle to fight if needed, self-defense. But through the cadence of her voice and the way her jaw settled in a thin line, clenched, I wondered for the first time whether the plan held no if for her, but only the tenor of when.

Tee never showed at school either, her desk empty next to mine in physics, all the locker room stalls deserted, where she sometimes hid to cut class. But Brett moved through the school halls, cocky swagger, indifferent gaze, and when we came to the bluffs that night, Tee was already waiting for us, silent, still.

Where the hell have you been? Wren asked, then her mouth closed upon her words when she saw the blood staining Tee's wrists, soaking through her sweatshirt sleeves.

Oh, Tee, I breathed, and moved to hold her. Kestrel looked down, away, as Tee pushed her palms rough against me.

Shove it, Teal, she said. Then she drew in a breath and looked at me, quiet. It's so much worse than you think, she whispered.

She told us no, they weren't cuts, no knives dug deep into her wrists, self-inflicted. They were from rope, rubbed raw. Brett had tied her to his bed. He'd bound her captive, over twenty-four hours, while he ate dinner downstairs, slept, went to school and sat in study hall, left her without food, water, to dig skin into twine to free herself, to thrash like some wounded animal.

I looked down past Tee's bloodied sleeves, saw a urine-soaked stain creeping down her jeans.

You don't know how humiliating, she said to us. You can't even fucking fathom.

She looked out across the bluffs, toward Brett's house, some unseen musty bedroom where he'd finally cut her free. I can't go home, she said. Not like this. She wiped her nose against her sleeve.

She stood and grabbed Wren's bat, leaning sturdy against a pine, and slammed it fierce into the picnic table bench. She picked up pinecones, cracked them hard out over the bluffs, jagged shapes black in silhouette against blue-green, northern lights streaked like finger paints down sky-dark canvas. And when she finally crumpled into the grass, collapsed on herself, shaking, I pulled her up and she let me. We left Wren and Kestrel behind, walked without words to my house where I climbed the tree and gave her my clothes, bandaged her wounds, let her light her old clothing on fire, down to ragged ash.

That Friday, after Wren's dad finally went to bed, we sat on her roof and watched the northern lights alone, just me and her, Tee sheltered in her bedroom and Kestrel refusing to walk from her house to Wren's. A fair reason, I knew, and why we never went to the bluffs on weekends, only week-nights, when bars closed early, when the streets were deserted. I could have pole-vaulted to Wren's, thrown stones through her window from mine. I could tiptoe across the street without the Jim Henshaws of Willow sidling alongside me, calling from cars.

That fucker needs a lesson taught to him, I said, thinking of Brett, then of Tee, her rope-cut wrists, how I washed them and her blood swirled down the drain, staining ivory porcelain pink.

You know what would happen, Wren said, staring out across her yard, eyes weary. Besides, that's Tee's problem. We've got our own.

I watched the dyed horizon, more crimson than blue tonight, and wondered if that was ever true, if any of us existed alone, our own separate spheres.

My dad, Wren said, glance burning down through roof shingles, he keeps that safe in his car. I saw him once. He put it in the glove box. All my cashed paychecks.

The auroras burned bright, shimmering lines, a beauty I knew blazed only from trapped particles, nothing more, ions shuttling toward earth, beating back, enraged that gravity held them.

I could take all that money, Wren said. I could just take it all back, if I knew he wouldn't beat the shit out of me.

I didn't look at her when she spoke, but I heard it anyway, that same cadence in her voice, something known when everything else for us was unknown, our fists the only solidity, the crack of knuckle on grain sack, a violence of choice.

Your mom, Teal. Wren looked at me. How is she?

She's tired. She gets by, I said, unsure why Wren brought her up. She never had before.

Wren sighed. Maybe once we're her age, these fucks will leave us alone.

I didn't respond, just watched the auroras, all those charged particles inside all that banded beauty as impossible to imagine as a future that far away, a future in Willow—and

Wren, even more impossible, a burn too bright to smolder, to sustain itself.

Tee hid her wrists when she came back to school, an easy task as October frosted into November, all our sleeves lengthened, and though her face was still bruised, patched black fading slowly to muted yellow, she told everyone she fell, slipped on a patch of early ice, not yet used to the care of stepping gingerly.

She forced herself to ignore Brett, we all did, but I saw her anger pool inside her, unchecked, watched her dig a pocketknife into her desk, deeper and deeper, chips of wood flaking, the center growing dark.

I took the back roads, cut through woods, wore bulky clothes, blended into pine. Jim Henshaw came by only once, dropped my mother off; he smiled at me and I turned away. My mother looked hurt, teenage apathy, self-absorption, but she squeezed Jim's hand anyway, told him thanks for the ride.

The auroras burned brighter, clear and fogless as the air grew starker and the solar winds more desperate. Wren's pay increased at the car wash, a brief burst of celebration we commemorated with beers, stolen cigars. She tried to hide the difference, kept some small cache for herself hidden between mattress and box spring, but when she met me in the street late, eyes red, dark circles, I knew her dad had checked the discrepancy against pay stubs, bruised shiner beneath her left eye sealing all certainty. She held a knife in her hands, small switchblade, extended.

When we reached the bluffs, Tee and Kestrel already there, throwing punches against pillows. Wren clutched the knife, carved a target into a maple tree. A silhouette, arms and legs, full height, taller than any of us. She stood back and stared, breath cloud rising, then stabbed the knife into the tree, hitting leg, abdomen, heart until the knife stuck, flush inside frozen bark.

Wren turned and looked at us, each of us, auroras glowing behind her, softening her somehow inside the rippled bands.

What did you want to be? she asked. What did you want, before all this, before you knew what we know?

Her words were general, spewed in anger, so swift and rapid I struggled to make sense of them. But I heard Tee breathe next to me, quick intake, the wind knocked from her as if she'd been punched.

I wanted a house, she said. Two dogs, maybe a cat. She glanced at us, eyes sad. I wanted to share that with someone who loved me.

Kestrel looked up, away from us, watched the lights shimmer blue-green, silent streaks. I wanted to be an astronaut. She laughed, mocking herself. Can you imagine? An astronaut. A girl from Willow.

That's more than me, Wren said. You know what I wanted? To cut hair. All I ever wanted, to open a goddamn hairdressing shop, and now, what? Not even scraps, not even fucking change, nickels, dimes. She stared at us. None of it, any of it, is mine.

Wren pulled the knife from the tree, retracted the blade.

If I left this place, that's what I'd do. If I just had the money, I'd leave this fucking place behind.

Tee nodded, Kestrel smiled with sorrow. And me, I watched the hard-packed ground, a question I'd never considered—if Willow had ever left me space to dream, to wish, or if I'd only had it so much better, my mother and me, no need for animal instinct, the inborn desire to flee.

In physics, Tee began to pass me notes, her arms stretched just enough for her sleeves to pull back, revealing scars, deep cuts scabbing toward healed. She passed me notes of houses. Drawings. Boxed figures, triangle on top. Circles of cats, of dogs playing in crude shrubs, herself standing there smiling, skinny stick-figure arms. I nodded, folded her notes into my pockets, paid attention instead to classroom lectures, to examples of vectors, momentum, power. Our teacher gave us equations, formulas that explained the charge of electricity, an endless stretch of theory never tied to tangible example, to the ionized particles above our homes every night.

I was studying on the couch when my mother came home, arms full of grocery bags from Al's Market where she'd stopped on the way, something she never did unless she had a reason.

Let's celebrate, she said, unloading tomatoes on the kitchen counter, garlic, onions, fresh produce she almost never bought, from-scratch meals she never made.

What are we celebrating?

She set the brown bags down. I don't know, she said. She stared at me, smiled. I guess I just wanted a nice dinner with my daughter.

She unpacked wine, giggled like she was fourteen, and I imagined her as a girl then, something I rarely thought about if ever—where she came from, what source, what roots of Willow sprang her from childhood, my grandparents gone.

I helped her make marinara, sliced tomatoes, celery, garlic. She let me have a glass of wine, asked about school, my friends. The scent of simmering onions filled the house, seeping into pillows, couch cushions, percolating warmth.

When we sat down at the table, I watched her twirl noodles into fork tines, pull them slowly from her plate, a comfortable silence between us, something earned.

Mom, I said.

She looked up at me, face smooth of lines, and the joy there broke my heart a little, to crack the silence, to pull her from the refuge of pleasure, so small.

What did you want? I asked. I almost couldn't look at her.

She twirled more noodles. What did I want when, sweet pea?

When you were a little girl. What did you want to be?

Her fork stopped twirling, and she set it down. She swallowed. A sadness wavered across her features, but when she looked up at me, I saw only a smile.

I wanted you, Teal.

She reached over, squeezed my hand.

In the end, you're my baby girl. That's all that matters.

She held her hand there on mine, then picked up her fork again, and I thought of the chemical plant, the sauce from scratch, small refuge of home while Willow crouched outside the door—if any moment of it, this life, was ever for her. I considered telling her about Jim Henshaw then, I wanted to open my mouth and shout all the wrongs, mine and hers, into the unsullied space between us. But the silence was too comfortable, her enjoyment too great, and the space sealed itself beneath the calm of the room, the warmth still leaking from the stove, beneath the joy on her face, cracked by sorrow if I spoke.

Tee and Kestrel were already at the bluffs when Wren and I arrived that night, Tee swinging the bat against the silhouette Wren had carved. Tee set the bat down when she saw us coming, picked up a pillowcase instead, and held it before me while Wren pulled out her pocketknife again, stabbed with precise force into the tree, targeted thrusts, focused accuracy.

It was me who first noticed when Kestrel never moved.

Kes? I asked, lowering my hands, turning her way. She sat on the picnic table, hunched away from us, sweatshirt sleeves pulled high over her hands, hood obscuring her head and face.

You okay? I walked over to her. You can take my place.

When I was close enough to touch her, I reached a hand out to her shoulder. She flinched beneath my fingers.

Kestrel?

I moved in front of her, felt my breath escape my lungs.

Swollen lips, crusted red. Damaged eye, bruise webbed down the capillaries of her cheeks. And in the glow I knew, could see the bloodied stain seeping down her jeans, ripped, staining the insides of her thighs.

I whispered Tee's name, then screamed, then screamed and screamed until someone's hand clamped hard onto my shoulder.

Jesus, what? Tee's voice, beside my ear.

Why didn't you say anything? I screamed. You were here. You were both here.

Tee stepped back, face splintered, confused. Then she saw Kestrel's clothes, her bruised face, bleeding mouth. I heard her breath accelerate, watched her lungs pulse, then heave.

Who the fuck did this? Tee yelled. Who did this, Kes? She looked at me. I didn't know, she said. I swear to fucking Christ, she was sitting here when I came. I yelled over, she yelled back. I picked up the bat.

I pulled off my jacket, wrapped it tight around Kestrel, a cocoon. I felt her body tremble through the fabric, small tremor burst to quake, burst to shuddering sobs, her mouth choking spittle, choking blood.

Wren came over behind us, switchblade in her hand.

Who did this?

Kestrel trembled, moved away from me, stepped off the picnic table.

Who did this, Kestrel? Wren repeated, voice level, harsh.

Kestrel stumbled back toward the woods, away from the bluff, away from the lights streaking the sky. In her few unsteady steps she hobbled, broken bird, unable to stand fully upright, barely able to walk.

Who did this? Wren shouted after her, voice echoing futility through the pines, since we all knew who it was, Kestrel's brother and his friends, and we knew knowing wouldn't matter, wouldn't pull the blood from her jeans, paste her cracked lips back together, rethread her ripped clothes, ripped heart.

Wren watched her go, while Tee ran after her, threw her arms around her, gently as she could, pulled her to the ground and held her, shaking. Wren stood there beside me, steamed breath escaping above her over the bluffs, settled against aurora, seashore green. Then she retracted the switchblade, dropped it heavily to the ground, and took off running, back through pine toward road.

I ran after her, mottled fear choking my chest, dread clouding, growing thicker. She ran back the way we'd come, through pines, across road, back over the sidewalks and gutters that had led us, each night, from our homes toward the bluffs. I followed, gasping air, chest burning frigid, night pulled in on lung. When we finally reached our houses, Wren disappeared into hers, and I stood on her lawn breathing hard, immobile, waiting for a light to blink on inside her father's room, for the same piercing thuds I'd heard so many times before, only now, something ending, something imminent.

But then Wren reappeared, glanced at me and glanced away, moved from her front porch to the garage's side door, slipped quietly inside.

When I finally stepped into the garage, Wren was sitting in the driver's seat of her father's Ford, engine off, lights extinguished, hands fixed tight around the thin arc of the steering wheel. I hesitated a moment, then slid into the passenger seat.

Wren, I said.

She stared ahead, her father's keys resting in the ignition, the glove box opened and waiting—she must have gone inside for every key. I knew he'd hid them, car key, deposit box key, Wren never said she knew where. The dread bloomed full swell in my chest then; this was it, her own plan kept quiet, crystallized, practice to performance, an end she'd always known.

It's bad, I said. I know. But it won't help Kestrel if we leave. It won't help any of us.

I'll pick her up. I'll pick Tee up. All of us, we can go. She looked at me. It's time, Teal. I can't stay here anymore.

I imagined her father waking up, car gone, money, safe box, daughter.

It's bad, Wren, the pay stubs are bad. But where would we go?

Her eyes flashed to me, burning through dark, through me.

You think I hate my dad so much about a bunch of fucking pay stubs? That's half of it, but it's nothing. She closed her eyes, turned away.

Well, what then?

Wren's lips closed tight on themselves, pursed to trap something in.

Your mother.

Her voice stopped there. A haze floated across my brain.

My mother what, Wren? What?

My father. She looked at me, anger faded for a moment, eyes widened in the shape of apology. He raped her, Teal.

The air of the car pulled the breath from me.

Wren stared ahead, eyes wet. He told me this summer. Said she was always so smug, there across the street, no man. Just fine with only her parents, no one else.

The car was a capsule sealed tight, smothering.

He told me in one of his rages. Smacked me across the face. Said he'd do it again, if I wasn't careful.

Wren's wet, red palm print, branded into wood. She'd known then, half-hatched plan, futile rage to pulse inside an eggshell of pines, for violence if needed, some space for us, some release. But for her, muscle to beat back if caught, only time to map the contours of escape. My chest seized, heart sputtering; my head swam through the years and years of asking about my father, who he was, where he'd gone and why my mother always turned away, deflected all question, said don't worry, sweet pea. I'm here for you. I'm always, always here for you.

Someone must have known, I said. Someone would have told me. I heard my voice growing louder. Why didn't you fucking tell me?

She touched my hand. I slapped it away. She sat back in the driver's seat, stared ahead.

You think anyone gives a shit here? Look at Kestrel. She can barely walk. Wren slammed her fists hard against the steering wheel. You think anyone will take care of her? Think anyone in this town gives a fuck?

Wren grew quiet then.

I'm sorry I told you. But we can leave this place. There's nothing here for us. Any of us.

I felt my nose burn, precursor to tears. I watched the dull walls of the garage through the windshield, and felt Jim Henshaw, Wren, her father, his past made mine, Wren's, ours together—I felt them all burn through me. I felt Kestrel, blood-soaked legs; I felt Tee, rope-cut wrists. I felt all of Willow, boiling burn, the smell of pine, the flash of solar storm, bands streaked from sky to ground where at the end stood my mother, four walls, her hand on my hand. You're my baby girl, Teal. I must have broken her heart not only to crack the silence of joy, but simply to make her say it.

I can't go with you.

Wren turned to me, face red as if struck.

I can't go with you. I can't leave my mother.

You could do whatever you want, Wren said, voice lower, already resigned. We could cut hair together. Until you figured what you want.

I didn't need to tell her I'd figured. I knew. I looked at her, roil within me; I wanted to slap her, beat back the words unraveled, shake some logic rattled through my hands to her, make her stop, make her stay. But I touched her face instead, hand held to skin partly mine, then pushed open the car door.

I walked across the street, stood on the front porch of the house that had always been my mother's and mine, had always been, still was. I sat on the steps, everything reeling, unsteady, and watched the shimmer above, fixed point, stable sky to hold me balanced. I heard the engine of the Ford ignite, the garage door roll up, watched the car back down the driveway, slow and quiet, rubber on pavement. Wren backed the car into the street, safely on road with highway ahead. Then she gunned the gas, tires screeching, smoldered rubber blazing a burn, particles unrestrained, streak like a hand held up in goodbye, scalded black. I watched her taillights fade until they became nothing more than a red glow sputtering out, until our street, our homes were what they'd always been again. Willow was quiet, unlit streets, darkened roads, everyone asleep. I thought of my mother, of waking her up, of pulling her onto the porch to watch the burn above, to see. I watched Wren's window, no flash, no Morse. I waited for dawn beneath the blaze, streaks so palette luminous I wanted someone next to me to watch a rage of electricity, magnetic storm, made beautiful only by collision, trapped, shuttling toward earth just to break apart.

IF EVERYTHING FELL SILENT, EVEN SIRENS

The first night we heard it, I slapped Tom hard across the face. The first time I'd ever hit anyone. The first time we heard a low howl, like distant wolves, only the sound came to us less warm-blooded, breathier, a sound like a soft siren, not human. Tom stood bent over the bathroom sink, eyes open and unmoving, clenching his nose as blood seeped in heavy droplets through his fingers, spat against porcelain, wet paint on blank canvas. I stood motionless, watched the blood—what vessels broke, how much liquid a body could hold. I stepped toward him, saw him flinch and felt my belly move, small somersaults. And then the sound through the bathroom window, ethereal hum, so low we thought we imagined it.

Tom stood, turned toward the window. Wrapped a tissue around his hand, held his palm to his face. I wanted to touch him, to feel some tenderness ripple through our separate membranes, smooth the razor inside me, to hold my hand against his skin. But he knew, as if we were one, as if his heart formed the other half of mine. He whispered *Don't*, a lone word to split a chasm, and in the slapped silence the sound outside filled the room, yawned through the bathroom window. A faint drone, not unlike slow-starting tornado sirens, the ones we'd heard all summer as storms swept across the Midwestern plains, a sound I knew even then I'd always associate with a taking away. The sound rolled over us, a wave, and I thought of my father then, touched Tom's hand, a point of contact he was too distracted to shun.

What is that? he said. He pulled the tissue from his face, stain of blood lining an edge of whiskers. He moved toward the window, peered outside. It's too late for sirens, he said.

I didn't know if he meant the hour or the season, but I looked too, over his shoulder, at the tree limbs of our backyard, gnarled dark in moonlight.

They wouldn't run the sirens at night, I said. The sound grew louder, whirling murmur, a distant chorus of some highway drone, and Tom turned when I spoke, as if just remembering I was still there.

I'm going to bed, he said, replacing the tissue against his face, moving past me, around the growing ball of my stomach, out of the bathroom. I followed him through the dark into our bedroom, curled toward him curled away from me, and tried to remember what it was we'd even fought about, my eyes closed, awaiting a sleep I knew would come in shallow fits, as it had all summer, as the hum threw its quiet weight against the stilled panes of our windows.

My father was a researcher, a renowned scientist on echolocation, the best man I ever knew. He'd grown gentler with age, due to many things, I'm sure, but I always assumed that dolphins had softened him, their playfulness, the primary locus of his life's work. He studied bats, shrews, various species of swiftlets for the ways their hearing patterned that of humans, but he owned a pod of dolphins at a research facility outside Columbus, Ohio, a place he regularly visited to study their navigational capacities though I knew, in the way he talked about his subjects, that there was more to this than biology.

There was a softness in him, a light that drew moths. A light I saw in Tom the first time I met him, something weightless and bright, a gravity sidling into the contours of my skin, a light to eclipse all moons. As a girl, my mother told me, you'll marry a man like your father, you'll be as lucky as I've been. I wanted to scream then, a revolt for rebellion's sake, in the same way I shied away from sciences, moved toward business, a material terrain over nature. And Tom, too: no facts or hard science but the freedom of the creative, a graphic designer, a man who captured light in mysterious ways. And yet even so, at my father's funeral, when my mother couldn't look away from his open casket, even then I never told her, never said how right she'd been, not even with a tiny pilot flame burning bright inside me, growing larger each day. Tom sat beside me, held his hand against my belly, and listened to the pastor, words my mother ignored for my father, the only light she could see in the room. All I saw were my mother's hands clasped together in her lap, her wedding ring visible, left hand atop her right—the way they rested there, alone, how they'd held my father's hands, how they never would again.

My father had cancer, slow battle, one that accelerated through the summer, one that hollowed us out beside his hospital bed in August. An unusual pattern of storms had circulated all summer, battering clotheslines, thrashing leaves, a pattern that carried us through hospital visits first, then brief stays, then a quick decline doctors told us to prepare ourselves for, as if preparation were possible. And then in late August, as we stood around my father's hospital bed, the sky darkened and the sirens escalated and when my mother stood to close the window my father exhaled his last breath, a sound like a sigh, like the wind that blew through the open windows before everything fell silent, even the sirens.

My father told me once that dolphin cries blared loudest, that their clicks of echolocation resounded higher than the decibels of blue whale calls, the gnashing of great white teeth, a sound to drown out the songs of every sea creature. I wondered what that would sound like, a sound loud enough to split an eardrum, louder than waves—or if it were quieter, a match for my father's voice, my baby's quiet kicks, a sound not unlike a breathy hum, its echo soft against our window.

Maybe it was the lumberyard, I told Tom when he finally came down the stairs, poured his coffee and ignored me. Maybe they're running the mills at night now, I said. Words that rang dumb in my own ears.

Tom stopped on his way back up the stairs, turned to look at me. The curve of his face swollen, just above the lip.

Can we talk about this? he said.

I studied the lines of wood in our kitchen table, swirls as complicated as fingerprints.

If it were the other way around, he said, you'd leave me. Can you hear me, Kate? You would leave me.

I didn't want to talk of double standards, or violence, or the hardened space between us that kept hardening though I knew we should, though Tom waited on the stairs for me, an apology I owed him. It was a weight too heavy, something ceaseless and vast, as terrible as a stretch of plains and blue planet without my father, a world that no longer held him but only me, everything I no longer was, a blaze smoldered to ash and still gasping to burn.

At work, my mother called. The PR firm cubicle I inhabited daily, unthinking, a job dulled to rote instinct and a lunchtime check-in my mother had grown accustomed to across the distended days of the past month.

They're negotiating what to do with the dolphins, she said. The lab. They want to sell them, maybe to researchers, but maybe to amusement parks too. Some SeaWorld bullshit. I heard her sigh across the line from their house in Columbus where she lived alone. Your father would hate that, she said.

Maybe he has a colleague, I said. What about Jensen?

Jensen studies bats. He's too busy at the lab anyhow, since your father passed.

Did you hear anything strange last night? I asked. Tom and I lived forty minutes outside the city, but I felt suddenly exhausted, talking about dolphins.

Nothing strange. If there was, I'd have heard it.

I knew my father had snored, knew its absence stilled the house in ways my mother found unbearable.

How's Tom? How's the wee one?

Fine, I said. They're both fine.

Babies think in logarithms, she said. Before they learn to count. Did you know that? The distance between one and two for them is like a lifetime.

I knew my father had told her this, his bevy of trivia, little details she let slide in passing but with fixed frequency now, letting him breathe the air through her. I'd wanted him to fill our daughter's mind with them, a childhood of facts, made to pull her toward the earth, to welcome her days to every wonder the world held. But the best we could do was let him go, just days after the ultrasound showed a little girl, my father knowing only she was on her way.

I didn't know that, I said, and felt shame wash over me then, a cascade.

That night, Tom stayed on the couch, watched television. I pretended to read, gradually lost interest, curled into the space beside him on the couch, felt him edge away.

They're selling the dolphins, I told him.

He didn't look at me. The blue television light flickered across his face.

My mother's upset, I said. No one at the lab needs them anymore.

Tom glanced at me, said nothing.

She asked about the baby, I went on. She probably thinks I'm not eating well enough.

And what did you tell her? Tom finally looked at me, straight on. Did you tell her that Mom punched Dad in the face last night?

I sat back, moved away from him.

Look. He closed his eyes. I know you're upset. I know how hard the past months have been on you. But we're having a baby, for fuck's sake. He glared at me. You cannot do what you did.

I knew that. I knew that, I knew that.

But I've never done that before, was all I could say.

I know, he said. You better never do it again.

And as he said it, the same howl seeped through the walls, as low and breathy as the night before, only closer, an approaching ambulance, the sound of swirling emergency.

———

As a girl, my father told me dolphins never really sleep. He said half their brain fall asleep, the other half in constant consciousness to watch for predators and to breathe. As I lay awake, listening to the hum, growing, settling like dust against our windows, I knew at last what he meant, knew it as well as I knew Tom's heartbeat near mine, slowed, asleep, the pattern of his breath as painful as an elegy.

I told Tom I was pregnant two weeks before my father's diagnosis. He came home with balloons that night, big gaudy congratulations balloons and triangle hats and kazoos and cake, our baby's first birthday party, the only one just for us. He pulled me close, kissed the line of my neck just below the hat's elastic, and I felt his light bloom from that spot, a light I thought of again and again in the following weeks as my father's began to dim.

That his light had left the earth was a truth, unbearable. It was something palpable, a feeling I'd never admit to my mother or Tom, a tangible lack I felt as clearly as the onset of winter, the sun turned from the earth, a rotation away that wore down my heart.

I thought I felt him again, only once, four days after the funeral, one morning after Tom left for the office. I was standing in the kitchen, bent over the sink and waiting for the morning sickness to pass. Our baby moved and then a cardinal hit the window, bright furious flash, a red as clear as a small star. *Look for me in rainbows*, my father had told us one July afternoon, when he felt something closing in upon him. But I saw him in cardinals instead, if only for a moment— and then he was gone, a bird flown away across treetops, as quickly and violently as it came.

———

In the morning, I awoke early, well before Tom. When he finally came downstairs, I'd already called in sick.

Baby nausea? he said. I thought we were past that now.

I'm just tired, I said. That noise again. It kept me up all night.

The lumberyard? He smiled at me, a smile that made him familiar again.

I don't know what it is. I can't believe you slept through it.

He sat down next to me on the couch. I'm sorry about the dolphins, Kate.

Each dolphin has a signature whistle. Did you know that? Scientists can tell every dolphin apart by the shape of their sonograms.

You sound like your father, he said. He touched my knee. A featherlight touch, warm and pooling, but to look at him felt impossible. His comment was one I'd have hated once, as irksome as wool scratching skin, but now his voice felt like a lullaby, some quiet, homesick hymn.

After Tom left I lay on the couch between sleep and waking, a sensation I imagined our baby felt floating inside the womb, muted pink light, the two of us dreaming together upon couch cushions. I knew her ears were taking shape, small snail shells, but that her eyelids would be closed for another few months, a world of sound but not light, only shadows and silhouettes and my movements.

I had wanted to be a biologist, once. I wanted to see the world as my father did, and my mother, retired now from teaching high school biology but there was a time, between the both of them, when our house flooded itself of wonder.

At dinner, over my head, they spoke of bottlenose dolphin behavior and fetal pig anatomy and cell division and plant species, so much that I yearned to know what they knew. But I trailblazed instead, set myself anew, and now even in dreams recognized the dull beat of hours, ticked away at my desk, as no match for the pulse of waves or blood.

In the afternoon, beyond fitful napping, I looked out the backyard window and noticed three neat piles of leaves as if they'd appeared for the first time. Tom had raked, clearly, had known how much I hated the upkeep of homes, even after the stretch of the summer when he'd picked up my slack and watered, mowed, weeded. I put on my jacket, started the car, and by the time Tom came home from work I'd gone to the store and returned and made homemade chili, his favorite.

What's this for? I heard him say, felt him come up behind me near the stove.

No reason. I turned and looked at him. Thanks for raking the leaves.

He kissed the top of my head, then leaned low to kiss my stomach, my sweater.

After dinner, my mother called. Tom answered the phone and I knew it was her by the lilting tenor of his voice, softened in her wake since my father left.

Where were you today? she asked when Tom passed me the phone. Did you go out for lunch?

Home sick, I said. Nauseous, and tired.

When I was pregnant with you, I ate fresh ginger. Grated it into tea.

That's not it, Mom. I hesitated, looked across the room to where Tom sat, reading a magazine. Have you not heard those noises at night? It's been so steady, the past few nights.

My mother grew quiet. No, dear, I've heard nothing.

It must be the lumberyard here, I said, an explanation that was beginning to sound thin even to me. So have you heard anything more? About the dolphins?

They found a buyer in Florida, she said. Some private facility that will charge people to swim with them. I'm going to see them tomorrow. They're being shipped out this weekend.

I heard the hurt in her voice, so palpable I could touch it.

Do you want me to meet you there? I can come by after work. Just tell me what time you're going.

No, she interrupted me, her voice quiet. I'll be just fine on my own.

When she hung up the phone, I blinked across the room at Tom, the stretch of hardwood between us vast as a valley.

They're selling the dolphins, I said. This weekend.

Tom looked up from his magazine. So soon?

My mother, she sounded so sad.

Tom set down his magazine, moved from the living room to the kitchen where I sat. Maybe it's for the best, he said, blanketing his hand over mine.

I looked up at him, his face unfamiliar, different.

How can you say that? I felt a white-hot prickling run the length of my body. How can you even say that?

Maybe it will help you both get closure, is all I mean. Why is that so terrible to say?

Because you don't understand, I said. I pushed myself away from the table and stood there a moment, blinking, wild-eyed and immobile, and then felt the air close in upon me, a vacuum, the space of the house too tight to breathe.

I walked out into the yard and watched the sun submerge itself into the silhouettes of trees, a goodbye that felt wistful as the wind picked up, swirled the leaves Tom had raked.

What the hell are you doing? I heard Tom's voice behind me, the crackle of leaves beneath his shoes as he approached. What is it that makes you so fucking angry all the time?

But there was no answer for him, no words, not even a deep well of rage to draw from out here on open land. Instead there were only tree branches, and wind, the swirl of air pushed from somewhere else on this earth.

There are rocks that slide across Death Valley, I told him, with no apparent cause of wind. Researchers know they move by the tracks they leave in the sand.

I don't know what to say to you anymore, Tom said. I don't know what the fuck's going on here.

Don't you? Jesus Christ, Tom. My father. My father's gone.

Sure, Kate, your father's gone. But something else is going on here. Why don't you tell me what the hell is going on.

The wind receded around me then, leaving only the red-blazed urge to strike, to hit him hard, the solidity of fist against skin. Before I could move the wind gusted back and slammed into both of us and then the howling began, a hum so loud it vibrated through bone.

Tom stared at me. Let's go inside, he said, the rage in his voice replaced by fear, and I moved through the door behind him, belly churning, the howl spinning a funnel cloud around us, so loud it seemed to rattle through my ears to my brain and then everything fell quiet, once Tom closed the door, the silence of the house as startling as a scream.

That wasn't the lumberyard, Tom said.

No. It wasn't.

I've never heard a sound like that in my life.

Neither have I. I moved upstairs to our bedroom, away from him, while the howl picked up again and rattled the windows. I didn't want to talk, not anymore, not for anger but for something more sobering, the first time I thought of them when Tom said it—of signature whistles, the only of their kind, and of clicks louder than waves, a sound strong enough to stretch across the sea, an unsounded void I once thought was the most immeasurable.

In the morning, after the sound pushed its fury against our windows through the night, after even Tom lay awake next to me, his breathing accelerated and after I tossed and rolled, our baby kicking, I awoke from some brief stint of sleep to the sunrise and no howl, its absence as violent as its blare. Over breakfast of only coffee, neither of us hungry, Tom looked at me across the kitchen table.

You need to tell me what's going on, he said.

I'd tell you if I knew.

But you know. You need to be open with me. We're having a little girl, Kate. I don't need to tell you that again.

I stood from the table, poured the rest of my coffee down the drain. This reminding of our child, the last thing I wanted to hear.

At work I tried to concentrate, despite sleeplessness, growing nausea, despite every tingling cell of my skin telling me to stop, turn off the computer, walk away and out of the office forever. When I'd first told my parents I was going into marketing, my mother's features fell. *But you're just like us*, she said, and I'd wanted to slap her in that moment—the only critique she ever lodged, as it turned out, the only moment she ever uttered words that weren't full-hearted support. It didn't surprise me that when the clock ticked past five, I found my car moving toward Columbus, toward my father's facility, where I knew she would be.

When I stepped into the facility, the one key I still had, I saw my mother at the other end of the pool, the high rafters of the ceiling splayed above her, dwarfing her small shape kneeling next to the water. The surface placid but for a few small waves, swirl of fins, several of six bottlenose dolphins my father had kept for over fifteen years. As a teenager I'd come to see them so many times, had sat by the water and held my palm to their noses though my father never let me swim with them, never wanted to commercialize them in any way. I'd been almost fearful of them, for the intelligence they held, for the things my father told me they could detect, as if they could see through me.

My mother didn't look up when I walked in and stood beside her.

I can't believe we're coming to the end, she said. Two dolphins swam past her. I couldn't tell if she spoke to me or to them. At last she looked up. Have a seat, she said.

I took off my jacket and shoes, sat beside her, let my feet sink into the water.

Back to work today?

Sort of, I said. Still no sleep.

My mother nodded like she knew, impossible to tell if she was remembering her own pregnancy or understood something more.

Mom, something's happening. These noises at night.

I stopped there, unsure where to go. She stayed quiet so long, watching the ripples, that for a moment I thought she didn't hear me.

In my class once, she finally said, we examined a case where researchers placed objects high on shelves, way above the hospital beds of people who were dying. Horseshoes, bowls, picture frames. The people who lapsed into comas, who needed crash carts, they could all describe the exact objects on those shelves when they woke up, though they had no way of seeing them from their beds.

A dolphin swam up to me, nudged my toes, so close I could barely breathe.

Your father always said dolphins were attracted to pregnant women, my mother said. Their sonar is so advanced, they know you're carrying a child before you do.

I remembered this, remembered my father telling me so. They can hear the heartbeat, I whispered. The dolphin pushed against my calves. I remembered they could detect illness as well—tumors, their sonar as intricate as ultrasounds. I wondered if they saw my father's cancer before he knew, a thought that pressed against my rib cage, the dolphin's skin against my skin. I wondered if they could see every hurt the human body held.

Tom is a good man, my mother said.

The best, I said, so soft I barely spoke.

My mother watched the dolphins a moment longer, the shadow of their shapes swirling just beneath the surface, and then stood. Still in rainbows, she said, and touched the crown of my head, though we both knew that wasn't true, that there was more, so many other iterations than refracted light.

On the drive home my belly moved, unusually active, not nausea or sickness. I wondered if our girl sensed the dolphins in the same way they sensed her, if energy could penetrate the walls of membranes just to be near unmediated life alone. I wanted that for her, an unsounded awe. To drive past shocks of turning trees and really see them, the blood oranges and sun-gilded yellows just outside my own driver's side window, to imagine where they came from, how they earned their crimson instead of the drone of some office, the dull slide toward numb.

As I pulled onto our street, the wind picked up again and whipped around the car, scattering leaves across the pavement. The sun began its descent beyond the trees above our house, casting the yard in muted light, a slanted glow that for a moment made the world warm.

Inside, Tom stood in the kitchen cooking pasta. He didn't turn when I walked in.

How's your mother? he asked, already aware of where I'd been.

She's sad. I set my keys on the table, felt something let go. And so am I.

Tom turned. Good.

I felt myself flinch. Good?

Good that you can admit that. That you can say it, finally.

I watched him, unblinking. And as he moved across the kitchen toward me, a blast of sirens erupted beyond the windows, the same sirens we'd heard all summer, the same sirens that brought only a heaviness now, a weight.

Tom stopped in the middle of the room and looked outside. I can't believe they're running those now, he said. The sky is clear.

I looked out the window too, saw only marbled sky and fading sunlight, but also the winds, tree branches bent beneath their force, an increasing churn that pushed at the windows until a parallel siren began to blare.

You know what that means, Tom said. A second siren, I knew, an emergency. A warning to move to the basement.

This is ridiculous. It's nearly November.

But the way Tom was watching me, I knew we should go downstairs, now.

I grabbed a flashlight, Tom pulled candles from the utility drawer, and we crouched inside the closet beneath the stairs, a sheltered womb, a space to shield us from wind and everything else as the lights flickered out.

You are sad, Tom said through the dark. You are sad and you can say that.

You don't understand, I said as the sirens grew louder. And then I heard the howl, low and faint, so distant I could almost ignore it.

I do understand, Tom said. The howl expanded and spread. And then he grew quiet and we both heard the sound growing louder, closer, felt it approach the concrete walls beyond the closet, half-submerged in the earth, a wailing cocoon enclosing the house.

My father, I said. To say the words was impossible, as if a lack of light stole the air from the room, as if the sirens pushed every shred of oxygen from the earth.

It hurts, Kate. I know. I know how much you hurt. But there's more, he said, and I wanted to push him from the closet, I wanted to sit alone in the dark and make him stop as the wind swirled around us, as the howl crowded the space between us.

That noise, I whispered.

I know. Just tell me. Tell me what else I need to know.

Our baby kicked against my belly, an energy vibrating to a pitch, and the windows of the basement blew open, a crash we heard clear from the closet, the wind ripping through the rooms and under the closet door, a current of air like a ghost.

I don't know, I said, louder. I don't know what this is.

But you do, Tom yelled back, his voice a match to mine above the wind, the screeching howl. You know as well as I do, you just don't want to say it.

I'm afraid, I said, and the howling exploded through my brain, so loud it seemed to topple the house, rip through every support beam, every blood vessel.

Yes, Tom said, a yell I barely heard across the clamor of wind and debris.

I thought of my father then, of a moment when I was small, when we'd walked down to the creek behind our house. He'd shown me a nesting pool of tadpoles, tails flicking, shiny glisten beneath the surface of a sun-speckled current. *Tadpoles have lungs just like dolphins*, he'd said and I watched until they floated to the surface, gulped what small breath their lungs could hold, a space I imagined as small as a pinprick, the size of the dandelion seeds I blew into the creek after my father walked away, back up the hill toward the house, the impossible wish to be everything he was, to know what he knew.

I am not who I wanted to be.

My voice, no louder than the faintest of footfalls. To say it was to break. But Tom heard it, above all wind and sound, above the blaring of howls and tornado sirens, the rattle of shutters and wind-splintered doorframes. I felt his hand through the dark, his palm encasing my own.

I am not who I wanted to be, I said again. For her. For anyone.

But you will be, Tom said. We all know you will.

I wanted to ask what we he meant, how he could possibly know, but the wind whipped the breath from my lungs, leaving behind only a wash of calm.

I held a hand to my belly, stomach subsiding, our baby somehow soothed. The lights flooded back on and the rattling ceased and the wind died down and retreated through the windows, undisturbed and unbroken, and the howl was gone, no hum, no light. The sirens slowed to a whine, then faded, then stopped. Tom pulled me from the closet to the window, where the sun sank the last of its light, a rotation away that broke my heart, even still, though I knew the warmth would burn elsewhere, some place unknown but bright. And then there was nothing, no siren, no noise and no emergency but only my belly, the shape of Tom's hand on mine, and the cadence of breath in the signature of our lungs.

A VERY COMPASSIONATE BABY

Gerard finds he cannot take his baby anywhere. Once, when they walked into the Dairy Queen on McPherson, a teenager passed them on the way out and dropped his strawberry ice cream on the pavement. The baby watched the pink scoop fall woefully to the ground, then exploded into such unmanageable tears that Gerard and his wife had to bring him back to the car. Another time, when they took the baby to the park on a sun-filled spring day, the park crew was out mowing the grounds, and the baby leaned out of his stroller, saw the grass flying, weeds razed, dandelion spores whipping up and away on currents of violent air, and he cried with such deep sorrow that the sun couldn't cheer him, nor the baby ducks swimming through the pond, nor the tulips blooming in the fields. They turned the stroller around and took him home.

And now, Gerard knows it for sure—that to take the baby anywhere is to risk perils like this, the startling onset of tears without warning, howls like alarms that alert every-one around them that something is terribly, terribly wrong.

When he takes the baby for a nine-month physical—after other similar incidents involving smashed ants, a broken jar of pickles, and a stuffed penguin, lost under the baby's crib for two days—he thinks to ask the pediatrician about the baby's behavior, in a way that won't sound strange.

"Dr. Mullens?"

She's bent away from him, weighing the baby on the child scale, but when he asks she turns, her face as blank as paper. The baby punches the air behind her, his tiny fists like clementines.

"What does it mean? If your baby cries a lot?"

She looks back at the baby, smiling and grabbing his feet.

"He doesn't seem overly tearful."

"Well, he isn't now. But I bet if you dropped something, like your stethoscope, he'd start crying. Probably immediately."

"You mean he's sensitive to loud sound?"

"No. That's not what I mean."

"Then what do you mean, Mr. Davenport?"

"I mean he cries, all the time, when anything happens that seems remotely sad."

"Babies mimic sometimes. Is that what you mean?"

Gerard sighs, looks around the room. He searches for anything, a demonstration, a way to show the pediatrician what he means. Finally he sees it—the wall of pamphlets, take-home brochures with titles like *Healthy Child Development* and *Could Your Baby Have Hearing Loss?* He takes one from the shelf, a leaflet about breastfeeding, with a woman cradling a child drawn across the front, and he waves it in front of the baby so he will look. Once he does, Gerard tears the pamphlet in half.

The baby stares. Then he bursts into tears, great heaving sobs, the halves of the leaflet limp in Gerard's hands.

Gerard looks at Dr. Mullens, who looks back at him and smiles.

"Well, Mr. Davenport," she says, rubbing the baby's belly, until his choking cries slowly disintegrate into sniffles, "it looks like you have a very compassionate baby on your hands."

She laughs, picks the baby up, puts him back on the examination table where he lies like a sack of potatoes, sniffles receding to sighs. Gerard looks on, feeling the awkwardness of dismissal, and wondering why, why in this room of all places, why is this funny, why would this ever be funny at all.

Just after the baby's first birthday, after a small party that Gerard and his wife consider a triumph, since the baby wept only a little when his lone candle was blown out, Gerard finds that the more the baby can toddle, the more he gravitates toward the backyard, toward its trees, the wide-open grassland they are lucky to have behind their home. As Gerard watches him meander through the grass, he imagines the baby must appreciate its solace, its expansive foliage, the way it rolls out like soft green carpet. And though Gerard has not said so to his wife, he imagines they both notice the baby's calm in the yard, how he laughs and plays, and how, despite the occasional tear over a torn blade of grass or a wilting wildflower, he is serene in a way that no longer seems possible elsewhere.

Because the baby is so peaceful, Gerard and his wife find that over time they develop a new habit of reading on the back patio, sometimes with iced tea or a bowl of mixed nuts, while the baby pokes around in the grass. Gerard knows when the baby wants to play, as he knew the first time, when he'd found the baby standing upright against the sliding door, tiny hands splayed against the glass, his solemn eyes fixed on the trees, the grass, the purple irises Gerard and his wife planted the year before. And now, each time the baby crawls toward the window, Gerard knows they can stand to read awhile, sitting on the back patio as the sun dips behind the trees.

One Saturday, Gerard sits on the patio eating a turkey sandwich when he notices the baby has stopped moving, lying motionless in the grass facedown, not crawling or poking his way through the lawn in the way he usually does. Gerard stands so quickly the sandwich tumbles in parts to the ground and he runs to the baby, imagining SIDS, imagining a once-pink face turned blue, all the quiet terrors a parent holds restrained until a single moment lets them explode.

But when he reaches the baby and turns him over, the baby smiles and giggles, hands clasped in what looks like prayer. Beneath him in the grass is a strange flower Gerard has never seen, something not unlike a dandelion sphere but more solid, substantial, something not easily blown away. When Gerard releases the baby from his grasp, the baby flips himself over, crawls slowly back, and lies motionless in the grass once again, eyes focused on the small, lone flower.

When Gerard's wife returns from her knitting club, Gerard is still sitting on the back patio, watching the baby lie rapt in the grass.

"He hasn't moved for two hours."

Gerard's wife sits down in the patio chair next to him.

"And he hasn't cried, either."

They watch the baby for a moment, neither of them speaking.

"Well, I think it's about time for his nap," she finally says, and walks over to the baby and picks him up. But when she does, he cries and waves his arms, and doesn't stop crying until she's settled him snugly in his crib, until the weight of drowsiness makes him forget.

They think it must be a fluke, one the baby won't remember, but later in the day, not long after he has awoken from his nap, he crawls toward the sliding door and looks somberly out on the lawn, his tiny brow wrinkled. Gerard looks at his wife. She looks back at him. They each grab their books without a word and take the baby out to the yard.

When Gerard's wife sets the baby in the grass, he laughs a little. As both of them watch, the baby stops and looks across the lawn, then crawls back to the flower, where, once he finds the right spot, he lies motionless in the grass like before.

"What do you think it is?" Gerard says, one Sunday as the baby lies in the grass, as he does almost every day with the flower, the only one of its kind in the yard, a spot the baby knows as birds know migration routes.

His wife looks over, then turns back to the morning business section, flips the page.

"What do I think what is?"

"The flower, honey. What else would I be talking about?"

His wife glances at the baby, lying on his stomach in the grass, feet kicked to the sky.

"You mean what kind? Oh, I don't know. It looks a little like an allium."

"No, not what kind. I mean what is it?"

"What is what?" she says, annoyed.

"What is it that's so special about that goddamn flower?"

His wife looks out across the lawn again, her face as even as porcelain.

"Maybe he likes it," she says. "Who cares? At least he's not crying."

She turns back to her paper and Gerard feels sheepish, a flush blooming across his face. But what he thinks, and what he wishes he didn't, is that maybe the crying was better.

The baby still cries sometimes, in odd moments when something goes awry, like when their server dropped a fork the other night at dinner, or when his wife accidentally washed a red sock with the whites and they all came out slightly pink. But for the most part the baby is serene, and Gerard wonders if it really is this flower, this strange, unanticipated bulb, that has quieted their baby with simple fascination, or if it might be something more.

Two weeks later, the baby is lying still and quiet in the grass when Gerard hears him shout something, a short burst that carries across the lawn.

"Riley!"

Gerard looks up, blinks toward the baby.

"Riley!" the baby shouts again, and Gerard pushes back his chair, yells through the screen door for his wife to come outside.

When she does, Gerard is kneeling in the grass, hunched over the baby, the round flower small but still visible, even from the patio.

"What is it, sweetheart?"

Gerard looks back at her and smiles, but something else colors his face too, something hazy and confused.

"I think he just said his first word."

Gerard's wife clasps her hands, runs out onto the lawn.

"Oh, really! What did he say?" Her smile is large, so large her lips part and her teeth peek out.

"I'm not really sure," Gerard says, and before his wife asks him what he means, the baby shouts again, over and over, Riley! Riley! Riley!

Gerard looks at his wife, and she looks back at him.

"What does that mean?" she asks, and Gerard shrugs. They both sit in the grass with the baby, with the flower, with this strange new word.

Later, after they've put the baby to bed and hear his rhythmic breathing through the monitor, Gerard rolls toward his wife, unsure if she's asleep, and curls himself into the curve of her back, sighs so she'll hear.

"Do you think he named the flower?"

"What?" She sounds groggy, like maybe she really was asleep.

"Do you think that's its name?"

"Oh God, Gerard, who knows?"

"Does it make you a little sad?"

His wife is quiet then rolls over, her forehead almost touching his.

"Sad how?"

Gerard's face reddens, though he doesn't know if she can see it in the half-darkened room.

"Sad like his first word wasn't mom. Or dad."

"Not really," she says. "Well, maybe."

Gerard stares at her, the panic in his chest creeping onto his face. "Oh, honey, don't worry about it." She puts her arms around him, pulls him close. "He'll talk to us soon enough. And besides, maybe he didn't even name the stupid flower. Maybe Riley lives on that flower, for all we know."

She laughs, kisses his face, and rolls away, but her words strike a new terror deep into Gerard's heart, the terror of maybe, of what if, the possibility she could be right.

For the next several days Gerard watches the baby, watches him lie in the grass as he has been, shouting Riley! every so often and clapping his hands, and though this is the only change, Gerard monitors it all with new suspicion, with mounting concern that maybe this Riley business needs to end.

The baby is happy, and didn't even cry the other night when he dropped a spoonful of peas on the floor, but Gerard can't ignore what his wife said. While they are sitting on the patio one afternoon, he looks over to see she's fallen asleep, eyes closed behind her sunglasses, and then he creeps over to the baby and hunches in the grass.

The baby barely stirs, doesn't notice anything beyond the flower, so Gerard leans far over the baby and peers down into the blossom, looks for any sign that things aren't quite right.

What he sees is nothing out of the ordinary, just petals, small filaments budding out in a sphere, stamens and pistils like any other flower. Though the species is one Gerard has never seen, its shape more like a globe, its stem thick and heavy, he looks down at the baby and sees the wide-eyed wonder painting his face and something within him relaxes, like piano strings loosened. He sits back on his knees and rubs the baby's tiny shoulders.

But just as Gerard pushes himself back, readying to stand, he catches sight of a small flash, something darting across the edge of his vision—something small and purple, quick like a flashbulb, scurrying through the flower's small filaments.

"Riley!" the baby shouts, and Gerard's panic is a broken dam pooling in the center of his chest.

"Honey, come over here!" he yells.

Within seconds his wife is standing over him, sunglasses still on.

"What? What is it?"

Gerard looks at her and can't think what to say, for its absurdity, for its blatant sabotage, for the way she will look at him when he tells her what he saw.

"I think something's living on this flower."

His wife's face goes blank. She doesn't reply.

"There's a Riley on this flower, like you said."

"Like I said?"

"The other night, when you said maybe something lives on it."

Her face tightens, like she's about to yell, but instead a smile spreads across her mouth, and she drops her head back and laughs.

"I was joking," she says. "Of course I was joking."

"But I saw something. There was something here!"

"Like what?" she asks. The baby giggles in the grass.

Gerard looks down at the flower.

"It was purple and small. I saw it, dashing around on that flower."

"Oh, for God's sake, Gerard." She runs a hand through his hair. "It was probably just a bug."

"I'm not crazy!" he shouts, pushing her away, suddenly angry, surprising himself with how angry he is. "Something lives on that flower!"

She stares at him, laughter gone. "Okay, relax. It's really not a big deal."

"A weird flower invades our yard, and suddenly our baby forgets who we are—that's not a big deal?"

She turns around, walks back toward the house.

"We can talk about this when you're calm," she says over her shoulder.

When she's gone Gerard stands there, the baby cooing and clapping at his feet, and wonders why, of all the lawns, of all the grassy backyards in their neighborhood, why of all homes did this flower take root in theirs.

———

When the baby begins to sniffle, a little summer cold, Gerard tells his wife it's nothing, but she gives him the look, the look that says maybe it is, and they strap the baby into his car seat and take him to the doctor. The baby is in good spirits, waving his arms and punching the air, but the farther the car moves from their home, the more rapidly his smile dissolves, until Gerard accidentally spills his travel mug on the car floor and the baby starts to cry.

At the doctor's office, the baby's weight, glands, pulse, his eyes and mouth are all checked. Gerard and his wife sit quietly out of the way on two stools while Dr. Mullens inspects the baby, checks his lungs and heart.

"Well, I think you're right," she says, examining the baby's nasal passages. "It looks like a cold to me, nothing serious."

"Is there anything we should do?" Gerard's wife asks.

Dr. Mullens clicks off her pen flashlight and tucks it into her front pocket.

"Just make sure he rests, gets plenty of fluids. If he's congested, use a rubber suction bulb to draw any mucus from his nose."

Gerard's wife looks at him, then back at Dr. Mullens. "Can he still play outside?"

"Like what kind of play?"

"You know, crawling. Toddling around. Just in the grass."

"That should be fine," Dr. Mullens says, her pen scratching against the baby's chart.

"And can he still play with the wood sprites and elves?"

Gerard's wife looks at him sharply, then looks away, embarrassed. Dr. Mullens glances up and blinks at Gerard.

"What are you talking about, Mr. Davenport?"

"Gerard, please," his wife says.

"I mean, Dr. Mullens, that our child has a new friend in the yard. It may even be why he's sick."

Gerard's wife sighs. "That's not at all why he's sick. My husband's just upset that our baby has befriended a flower."

Dr. Mullens blinks at them. "It's okay for children to play. Lots of babies have imaginary friends."

When he hears this, what Gerard wants to say is that no, it's not imaginary, that he's seen this "friend" with his own lucid eyes. But he smiles instead, a thin, reedy smile, and says, yes, of course it's okay for children to have make-believe friends.

Everyone is silent on the car ride home, including the baby who, despite one brief tantrum over a stop sign he sees out the window, dilapidated and half-bent to the ground, sleeps soundly until the car whirs softly back into the garage.

Inside, Gerard's wife cleans out the baby's nose, then hands him to Gerard and retreats to their bedroom. She hasn't spoken since they left the doctor's office, and Gerard wonders if she intends for him to take the baby outside, or if the baby should rest and nap. But the baby crawls to the window, stands on shaky legs and murmurs toward the yard, and Gerard sighs, thinks no, for all they know the flower has in fact caused the cold, so he pulls the baby back, curls him into his arms, and sits looking down into his small face.

"Not today, little man," he says, and the baby shouts, then howls, sobs growing louder like an ambulance siren approaching. Gerard rocks him and bounces him on his knee, but he just keeps screaming, eyes squeezed shut, nose running, until Gerard's wife yells from the bedroom, just take him outside, just let him see his flower.

Gerard exhales, stands. He opens the sliding-glass door.

The baby finds his spot quickly and lies motionless in the grass, sobs subsiding into coos. Gerard stands watching him, hands at his sides, then turns back to the patio and glimpses for a second his wife in the window, peeking out from behind their bedroom curtains.

Gerard situates himself in a patio chair, no book, no magazine for distraction. He closes his eyes, lets the late-afternoon sun warm the tops of his eyelids while the baby's giggles drift past him on a light wind. He breathes out and lies back, knowing his wife is probably watching. But then he hears it, the baby's shout, not Riley now but something else, something new, something that jolts Gerard from his chair.

"Rufus!" the baby shouts. "Rufus! Riley!"

Gerard sits up, stares across the lawn where the baby is laughing and kicking his arms and legs, almost like he's swimming across the grass. Gerard pushes his chair back and runs and when he reaches the baby, he kneels down. And what he sees, there in the center of the flower, is a sight like a shockwave through the currents of his heart, not one but two purple orbs, flashes like heat lightning darting across the bulb's surface.

"Oh, no," he says softly, then louder as the tiny sparks keep moving. "Oh, no, no, no! Absolutely not!"

"Rufus!" the baby shouts.

Gerard looks at the baby, then back at the flower, then over his shoulder at the house. And before he can temper the impulse with reasoned thought, his hands grab the flower's thick stem and he rips, pulls, he screams as he tears the bulb from the ground.

The force throws Gerard onto his back in the grass and then there is quiet, no sound, a calm breeze passing over Gerard's face as he stares at the pale sky, the flower clenched in his fists like some weed. It's so peaceful that for a second Gerard thinks it's a dream, that maybe he didn't pull the flower out by its roots, that maybe the baby is lying in the grass with him, asleep, that maybe they are napping to fight off his cold.

But then it starts, a low moan, which grows and swells until the baby is screaming like Gerard has never heard, like every travel mug and every ice cream cone and every stop sign in the world has been demolished. Gerard rolls onto his side and cradles the baby against his chest but the baby keeps screaming, until at last Gerard's wife runs out to the yard and looks from Gerard to the baby, to the flower, and back to Gerard.

"What's this?" she asks. She looks like she could cry.

Gerard looks away, then back up at her, knowing how pointless it would be to lie.

"I can't believe you just did that," she says, and though her voice is even and still, Gerard recognizes an undulating blaze beneath it, rolling water on the verge of boiling.

She picks the baby up and walks away, back into the house, his wails as deep and desolate as foghorn blasts, and Gerard understands the sound now as familiar, resurrected, as it will be when the baby sees their neighbor trip on the way to the mailbox, or when his wife accidentally drops an ornament as she carries it to their Christmas tree, or when their garage sale sends old dishes and broken appliances, discarded and unwanted, to other people's homes far away.

"I did it for him!" Gerard shouts after her. "I did it for his own good!"

But when he looks down at the flower, lying askew in the grass like carnage, he wonders if this is true, if it were ever true, and if the baby will remember this at all once he's grown, with no flower to recall and only a world of sadness before him, its sorrows to keep like gemstones, to enfold in the pockets of his small, vast heart.

MINIVAN

Jane hovers in front of the mirror sometimes, when she thinks I'm not looking. Tweezers in her left hand, a mat of hair raised in her right, she homes in on a single gray strand nobody can see, laid low against her scalp, a needle in the haystack of her dark, heavy waves. She plucks the colorless ones, releases them into the trash can below our bathroom curtains, sometimes with brown strays she's carelessly removed. When she's satisfied, she replaces the tweezers in our medicine cabinet, next to my razors and aftershave.

Two of her gray hairs stick to the curtains, silvery white against the muted green fabric, and I study them as I brush my teeth, something I used to do while walking around the apartment, making the bed or putting dishes away, but Jane tells me now that this makes her nervous. It's annoying, she says, like pacing. So I hunch over our cramped bathroom sink, my mouth all foam in the tiny vanity mirror, and maintain perfect eye level with the hairs, two stragglers that floated the wrong way on their slow journey down.

In the bedroom Jane huddles against the headboard, knees pulled to her chest, a pair of noise-canceling headphones hugging her ears. They are mine, a set I bought just after college when we lived in a boxlike studio together, nearly three years ago. I used to plug them into the television when Jane wanted to read in silence. The headphone cord snakes from the sheets across the carpet to our stereo, and this trend of hers is also new, something I'd have noticed earlier if she let me pace around, brushing.

I curl up beside her, tap her shoulder. She turns, her cheek soft against my hand, and pulls a speaker back from her ear.

"These are nice, Jon," she says. "They drown out the world."

Before I can answer, she pulls them off and turns out the light.

"It's like I'm not even here," she says through the dark.

A month ago, when the early May sun at last banished all snow from Chicago, Jane started a garden. I found her standing with her cereal, scrutinizing our feeble patch of patio grass, and two days later she'd dug up a small square in the farthest corner of our already-small lot, her palms and knees black with loam, hiding scars that were just beginning to heal. Not a real garden—just two small cherry tomato plants, marked by stakes she hoped they'd climb. She nurtured them inside first, seating them in the living room as we watched old movies, then transplanted them outside, showered them with water. She gravitates that way now, nearly every day after we eat dinner. I've asked her if she wants help, but she always shakes her head no. And I don't push this—I can't—in case she thinks I see her as victim like everyone else does, as someone who can't save herself.

When I come home late from school, after an exhibit to let the parents to see what their kids have been working on, Jane is sitting in the living room, feet propped on our otto-man, shins stained pink with calamine lotion.

"Poison ivy," she says, reaching forward to scratch. "The tomatoes were a bad idea."

I glance out the window, see her cherry tomatoes are just starting to appear, small globes like pale green gumballs, weeks from blooming to ripe.

"I don't know about that." I sit beside her, inspect the bright red bumps poking up from the lotion. "This will go away. You'll have tomatoes all summer."

She leans forward, like she doesn't hear me. "I wish I could graft skin," she says. "I wish I could scrape this rash right off me." She looks at the bumps. "Motherfuckers."

Her fingers clench, her nails extend. I nudge her hands aside before she can scratch the flaked pink away.

Jane asks about work, what parents said about this round of paintings. She even asks about Toby, her favorite student of mine, the smallest boy in the second grade with the big-gest pair of glasses. She thought he was precious, so small he could fit in her pocket, the times she stopped by on her days off from the salon to see what I did all day. She hasn't come by at all for summer session, hasn't wanted to be around the kids, their collages, their colorful fingerprints smudged into the rough texture of the paper. She hasn't asked about Toby in almost two months.

I haven't brought this up, or anything else, and won't un-til she is ready. But I've seen her look away when we pass strollers on the street, or when children stand before us in the grocery line, pulling Mars bars from the convenience shelf before their mothers can stop them. I've seen her watch them, her tongue moving across the chip in her left canine, the one she hides now with close-lipped smiles so no one will ask.

We haven't gone to the movie theater for the past two months. We went only once, back in April, to take her mind off the wave of lineups the police put her through, after she decided to prosecute against their advice. But when the lights dimmed and the previews began, I heard her breath accelerate inside the dark. When I reached across the seat, I found her fingers gripping the armrest. She whispered that she might faint, and we left before she could. The darkness is what it was. So much dark, like so many sidewalks unlit by so few streetlamps.

I ask Jane how her day was, but she brushes off the question and watches her blossoming rash instead, says client flow has been slow lately. Summer vacationers, people letting their hair grow wild in the warmer months, though I wonder if her boss has lightened her load, a gradual ease back to work after taking last month off. Jane is the reason I haven't paid for a haircut in over five years, but even this has gone by the wayside lately. My head feels overgrown, shaggy in the back by the ears, but to ask her now for this favor, it feels horribly frivolous. It can wait until August, when the new class of kids comes in, and by then enough time will have passed. By then, summer's unbearable fluidity will have browned into the crisp edge of fall, and a new season will maybe feel like a new life.

After dinner, Jane spends most of the evening outside— not gardening, the patch is still too small, but reading, though each time I look out the window she's watching the sky instead, a nightfall bereft of stars. She stares into the black, darkening heavily above a tinted horizon, and reaches forward every so often with fingers extended above the rash, like she wants to scratch her legs raw.

I mentioned last month that maybe she should see a therapist. I said it gently but meant it with resolution. Therapy seemed like a requirement. But she glared at me and turned away, and said over her shoulder, mouth muffled into skin, *But I was just walking by. They should be in fucking therapy, if anyone is.*

I am reading in bed when she finally comes in from the yard. I hear the screen door open and close, and then she is nestled into the sheets beside me, her head resting on my shoulder, the headphones discarded on the floor at least for tonight.

"Breastbone," she says, her palm laid flat on my chest.

It's something she said once after we'd just met, the first time she ever touched me in a way that wasn't platonic. We were lying on my bed when she reached over, placed her hand on my sternum and said it, *breastbone,* and the shape of that word in her mouth felt like that spot had barely existed until she named it.

Her hand stays on my chest even after she falls asleep. And this, these glimmers, like stars falling through the dark until they disintegrate—this is what I cling to, to know the Jane I knew is there.

A week passes before she brings home a gun. It is there on the kitchen counter when I return from work, a Glock I look away from when I imagine her palms enclosing its rough grip. She mentioned this possibility just once, when we were walking home from the park last month after dusk and she slowed her pace along the sidewalk, looked off toward the lighted windows of apartments above the storefronts we passed. She wanted something reliable without intricate parts, something uncomplicated that would react immediately if the need arose. I told her then that it made me uncomfortable, that she didn't need a gun, but the one word I should have said, the one suspended all these weeks above the permit fees, the background check, the paper-work she must have completed without telling me, is the one I can't say to her now. No. That word has fallen from my mouth, like too many ice cubes, overcrowded by the implication of what it could mean inside the snail-shell chambers of her ears.

Jane walks in from the living room, and for just a mo-ment she is an intruder and this is her gun, a disorientation that prickles down my arms. She's never home from the sa-lon before I return from school.

"I took the afternoon off," she says. Her hands find the countertop, just inches from the grip, and I look away again. I don't know what to say.

"Look, I know you disagree." She sighs, as if I'm a parent who's taken away her driving privileges. "That's why I didn't tell you."

A quiet cloud rolls into my brain when she says this, some muddled rage with no source, no culprit, not her or me though we are here, as if on the other side, a new world where we make decisions we never dreamed of and Jane buys a gun while I teach my class of second graders how to wa-tercolor.

"So, what?" I try not to yell. "You're going to carry this around with you? A gun-slinging straight shooter?"

She looks at me and her eyes burn the way they did when I first walked into the room at the hospital, a wind-whipped, bitter morning just past the official start of spring; when they finally let me see her, after the nurses gathered the kit, the samples and scrapings and swabs she still hasn't talked about, and at last helped her shower.

I tell her I'm sorry, drop my workbag to the floor and move around the counter, place a hand between her shoulder blades. She leans into my chest, and over the top of her head I can see my hand, there on the fabric of her shirt—small-seeming, insignificant, no better protection than a wooden spoon, not then and not now.

Jane stays inside after dinner, resists the pull of the tomato garden, the firm bulbs crimsoning pea green to scarlet, and sits beside me on the couch, her hand skirting my stomach. These small affections, our shared convergences, they are enough for now because they must be. We haven't made love much at all since April, only once or twice in cautious movements, and she softened into sobs each time, her broken tooth biting her lip, slow tears as if she didn't want to hurt my feelings, to say this wasn't right.

I want to tell her I'm not them. I want to tell her I am safe. But I hold my breath; those words seem useless, they are things she must already know, of course she knows. She knows more than I'll ever know.

People have asked me how I feel, *Oh you must be so angry,* in moments when Jane isn't around. And I nod, tell them yes, and change the subject with a different kind of anger, that they expect me to be anything at all. Because the truth is that I feel close to nothing. No anger, no impulse for revenge, no restless twinge of retribution, no baseball bats tucked into my trunk. What I feel instead is helpless, completely inert and static, like her motions and movements are things I should have guarded more carefully, and that negligence will blanket me forever like a fine, irremovable powder.

I also wonder sometimes, when I look at Jane across the dinner table or while she's asleep and I'm not, if maybe I can't believe this, that it actually happened. I knew of violence but not random, unchecked brutality, a violence that makes me sorry to inhabit this world, to know the impulse exists. She was just walking home, the three blocks from the blue line to our apartment. Eight at night, the late March sun gone, but the sky wasn't even fully black when they screeched up in a minivan, the one grabbed her and shoved her in the backseat, the other held the wheel. It must have taken seconds, not long enough for anyone to notice, but they drove around for two hours, taking turns, and when they finally pushed her from the van, somewhere south in a residential neighborhood, a middle-aged man found her unconscious on his lawn and called the police.

That's all I know. I don't push it, not past this brief nutshell the cops gave me, after I called them when she never came home, never answered her phone, after they called back that she'd finally been found, that she was at the hospital and I might want to sit down before they told me what happened.

People have asked, *Don't you want to know?* My colleague Tim, he said over lunch about his ex-girlfriend, *When Susie fucked that guy from her gym, I wanted to know everything about it. How many times, whether he fucked better than me, what kind of mattress and where, or if they just tore their clothes off in the goddamn car.* I'd thrown out my half-eaten lunch, the world he lived in so far apart from mine. I told him to go fuck himself, something I regretted later in case my students had overheard me.

Jane says she'll keep the gun inside, that she won't carry a concealed weapon in her purse. I wonder what the point is, if she never felt unsafe at home. But as we sit there watching television and Jane shoulders herself deeper against my side, I think I see it exactly from her eyes. I was the safety of home, a protection that failed. I was made of unreliable parts.

Jane pushes herself up from the couch, and I avoid her eyes, watch her shins instead. Her rash has died away to a visible redness without the itch, and for a moment there is comfort in this, that the passage of time can transform and remove.

"It's late. I'm brushing my teeth." She turns off the television. "I'll be in bed in a minute."

On my way to the bedroom, though the bathroom door is half-closed, I can see her inside hovered low and squinting deep into the mirror, her tweezers suspended above her head to purge what doesn't belong, hulking unseen beneath the hairline.

At school, Toby asks where Miss Jane has been. He asks offhandedly, while dipping strips of newspaper in paste and cementing them to a balloon, but the feigned nonchalance of children lets me know he misses seeing her. For a moment I want to pick him up, to forget the rules of classroom conduct and pull his small face to mine, tell him he is wise and how much we share. But I nod at his papier-mâché instead, tell him he's on the right track, and say Jane has been sick but she'll hopefully come by soon. Toby looks up at me, and through his thick glasses I can see why Jane has stayed away. Toby knows I am lying.

This week we are making piñatas, and each student has blown up a balloon to paste with newspaper, to paint as clowns or planet earths or cartoonish self-portraits. So far two kids have whispered concerns to me about leaving a hole big enough for candy, once we pop the balloons. Sam worries he'll forget to leave an opening entirely, and Caroline thinks that Snickers bars, her favorite, might be too large for her tiny gourd-shaped piñata.

While the kids color as they wait for their balloons to dry, Althea approaches my desk and asks if it will be hard to paste the hole shut, once the candy is safely inside. When I look up and see the anxiety creased between her eyebrows, I wish with every strand of my stretched-thin heart that I was her, if only for a moment. But when I see her knotted knuckles, clamped hard around her paintbrush, the feeling passes. I tell Althea we will seal the piñatas the same way we made them, once the papier-mâché has dried, and that there is nothing to worry about.

On the subway home I think about Jane's gun. She keeps it in her bedside drawer, claims she barely knows how to pull a trigger, but that she'd know if the need came, she'd be ready this time around. A flood of passengers enters the train, and when I move over a seat to let an older woman sit down near the aisle, I catch my reflection in the subway car's panoramic windows. July is halfway gone, and the new students will be arriving in just a few more weeks. My hair is longer than I thought, unruly and disheveled.

Since Jane won't be home for another hour anyway, I stop by the Super Cuts a few blocks from our apartment. Jane claims places like this are what made her a stylist, after one incident in particular when a Fantastic Sams cut bangs to her hairline. But what I need is simple, a trim straight across. Just enough for presentable parent-teacher conferences in August—nothing someone here couldn't do.

A stylist seats me in front of a mirror and begins trimming away, dipping the comb in water every so often to straighten the strands.

"You've got split ends." She meets my eyes in the mirror. "Been awhile since you've had it cut?"

And all I can do is nod, before she pushes my chin down to trim the back.

At home, the tomatoes have ripened into bright red gum-drops almost overnight, so I pull four from their vines, to surprise Jane and show her the garden wasn't futile. The poison ivy near the plants has receded, so far that Jane could even plant more vegetables if she wanted, maybe mums or squash for fall.

The tomato salads I've made are ready when Jane walks through the door, sets her bag down, and sits at the table. I start to tell her about the piñatas, the kids' worried questions because I know she'll laugh, and the roster for the new semester. I want to tell her too that Toby asked about her, but I hesitate before the words come.

It is only when I set the salads on the table that I notice she hasn't responded. She is staring at me instead, her mouth set, eyes tapered into slits.

"You got your hair cut," she says.

"Well, yeah. For the fall."

Jane's jaw shifts beneath her skin. "Why didn't you just ask."

"You've been busy. I didn't want to bother you."

"Bullshit, Jonathan." My full name, only when she is furious.

"It's just a haircut," I tell her. "Really, it's not a big deal."

"Oh, my poor girlfriend." Her voice mocks mine. "My girlfriend's so fucking fragile that I won't even ask her for a haircut, the same goddamn haircut I've had for years and years."

The room falls quiet between us, a silence with space for me to begin to understand.

"Do you know what the police asked me, before you got there?"

I don't know what to say to this. We are characters in a flipbook; we've switched scenes entirely.

"Why were you walking home alone, a pretty girl like you?" Her voice is mocking again. "You city girls and your sundresses, you always think you can take care of yourselves."

She's never told me what they said, or anything else about that night. I step closer to her and she steps away.

"You want to know what happened to my tooth?" She grins at me, but it's not a smile. I can see the chip, its jagged void. I shake my head no. There is nothing I want to know less. "I punched the first guy in his goddamn face, when he tried to push me down. That's when he slammed my face into the car window."

These are things I cannot hear. These are things I will think about in detail, for days and months and years.

"I saw that minivan again." She is staring at me. Adrenaline tingles, explodes through my arms. "I saw it again two weeks ago. I wanted a gun before the police would ever do anything about it."

"Why didn't you tell me?"

She hears me though my voice falters, though I barely speak.

"Because you're no different," she says, and my heart is an egg, shell fragile hiding yolk, more fragile than she'll ever be as she moves past me and out the door.

I am in bed, listening to my headphones that are now hers, when I hear her come home. The volume is low though I want to hear it anyway, this retreat from the world, lights out so I understand the same darkness. But when Jane walks into the bedroom, she flips on the light and stares at me. Her face indicates some threshold, like she wants to tell me something or I should begin first.

"That haircut sucks," she finally says. She approaches me tentatively, then grabs my wrist and leads me to the bathroom.

Once I am seated in a chair, over bathroom tiles for easy cleaning and she's sprayed my hair with water, Jane moves around my head determining how to shape it, how to fix this devastating mistake. She doesn't speak to me, doesn't even look me in the eye but concentrates instead, her chipped tooth biting the edge of her lip.

"Tell me about the minivan, Jane."

"The lineup is next week." She snips hair from my temple, her voice short and terse. I feel her hesitate, then she starts trimming again, quick. "If it's them, I'll get rid of the gun."

She says this offhandedly, a small step in my direction.

"I'll go with you," I say. Her fingers hug my scalp but she continues to cut, a focused professional with no space for dialogue, no room for error.

I want to tell her I've failed her. As she moves around my head until she is standing in front of me, scissors held above my forehead, I want to tell her I am sorry, for all my mistakes and theirs, the hospital and the police and the faults of men. I will eat every single mistake until there are no more left; I will swallow them so she is safe, no guns and no minivans, no sidewalks and no darkness. But when I look up at her and she finally meets my eyes, there are no words for how the world has lost her.

Because there is nothing else, I reach my hand out to her chest.

"Breastbone," I say.

She holds my eyes for a moment, then looks away when hers begin to brim.

So she can concentrate again and finish the haircut, I tell her Toby asked about her today, to lighten this space and help us forget. She is so quiet I think maybe she hasn't heard me, but then she laughs a little and the sound spills through the bathroom, a sound like marbles, as though we are children again.

"Toby," she says. "I'll have to come see him soon."

When Jane finally completes the haircut, she stands back and observes my head. Her expression is the same as when she inspects her own scalp, like she's looking for the faults, the hairs that don't belong. But when her eyes move down and meet mine, her face softens and for a moment we are who we've always been, small as a seed, a moment where we begin.

NOT FOR GHOSTS OR DAFFODILS

After Ben Mortimer's wife left him, and after he sat his daughter down to say her mother wouldn't be coming back, Maple took her blankie and hid under the bed for three days. Ben called in sick and worked from the child-sized desk in her room, bringing crackers, grape juice, and Twizzlers to the edge of the dust ruffle every so often, all of which were pulled beneath the fabric by a small hand.

Grace had said she wasn't happy, that she didn't feel like a mother or wife, that her own life expanded far beyond her, some unexplored terrain. And though Ben pleaded, though he'd gestured upstairs toward their still-sleeping daughter's bedroom, Grace turned away, moved her eyes from her packed suitcase to the driveway beyond the front window where her car sat idling, to take her where, she couldn't bring herself to say. Ben thought of this, of her audacity, that Grace—*grace!*—could leave so inelegantly, so abruptly, and he stabbed his fingers into the computer keypad atop Maple's small desk. Right in the center of a company report, he typed a list, the clacking of which stirred Maple under the bed; he heard her shift, repositioning herself beneath the quiet cloak of box springs.

YOU ARE:
The nerve of chewed bubblegum, clinging to shoes.
A black stain of coffee, darkening teeth.
As bad as mother rabbits, once their babies touch human hands.

Maple sighed below the bed, and Ben saw the bed skirt move, puffed up in her exhalation of breath. He lowered a juice box toward the dust ruffle, and Maple reached out her tiny fingers, pulled it under.

On the third day, after Ben had switched from sliding snacks beneath the bed to full meals, Maple crawled out and stood blinking at him, a swirl of dust bunnies clinging to her hair.

Ben took Maple back to preschool, her days of cloistered mourning apparently over, and returned to work, a non-profit organization where he hid inside his office to avoid the inevitable questions, brows scrunched in concern. But at home, after Maple went to bed and Ben retreated to his study to immerse himself in fundraising reports, she developed a new habit, one that showed itself when Ben thought she'd finally fallen asleep.

"It's raining bugs."

Ben looked up from his desk, saw Maple's round face peering in at the door.

"Raining caterpillars! Inchworms everywhere!"

Ben sighed and pulled off his glasses. He picked Maple up and took her down to the kitchen, poured her a glass of milk, and sent her back to bed, once he'd checked every window in her room to make sure no insects fell from the sky.

After similar incidents on following nights—a frog soaring across her room on lily-pad hovercraft, an oak tree in the yard screaming so loud she couldn't sleep, a talking spider spun down from her ceiling fan—Maple padded into the office and stood there sucking her thumb.

"I've caught a ghost in a jar."

Ben heaved a breath, stared at Maple's toes peeking out from her small nightgown.

"Want to see it?"

Ben took his daughter by the hand, and she led him to her bedroom where an empty Mason jar stood on the nightstand. Where she'd even found it, he had no idea.

Maple moved toward the nightstand, held her face to the glass. "Her name is Harriet."

"How do you know?"

"She told me." Maple tapped a moon-shaped fingernail against the jar.

"What kind of ghost is she?" Ben felt tired.

"She's a bright yellow daffodil."

Ben sat down on Maple's bed. His brain hurt. He'd heard of imaginary friends, of friendly phantoms. But never the ghosts of flowers.

After he read Maple a bedtime story, pushing the mason jar farther away on the nightstand so she would forget it and sleep, Ben turned off the computer and settled into his own bed, its shape strange to him, a two-man rowboat now unmoored, adrift with one. The sheets on Grace's side lay smooth as the flatline breaking sea from sky, and Ben rolled away and faced the wall, teeth clenched, eyes shut. You have abandoned ship, he thought.

YOU HAVE:
Cancelled your pacts, with me, with her.
Left no instructions.
No idea what this is like.

Maple carried the ghost with her everywhere. To the breakfast table, where she set the jar against the window, so Harriet could soak in the solidity of sun. To the bathtub, where she flew Harriet around like a rocket above her while Ben scrubbed shampoo into her mess of curls. Maple even brought the jar to school, which Ben allowed warily, so long as she kept the container in her backpack. Ben looked on with vigilance, unsure what this ghost, this daffodil meant to his daughter, but her nighttime awakenings had stopped, her fanciful stories subsided, so Ben let Maple proceed, let her pour water every so often into the jar to replenish Harriet's wilted, invisible petals.

Ben progressed as usual at work, put together files on the organization's major donors, sipped coffee through the afternoon and tried not to think of Grace: his phone silent, no midday calls from her as there once had been. He'd promised himself not to look her up, though the research he compiled made possible such things—property values of prominent patrons, their political donations, their family history and social involvements. But he promised he wouldn't do it, that he'd move about his days, that he and Maple were better off without her, without a woman so easily budded to full bloom without them.

But when he picked Maple up from preschool and tucked her into the backseat, her report of the day made him waver, reconsider.

"I saw a pink dolphin at school."

Ben watched his daughter in the rearview mirror, where she stared back at him, eyes big as golf balls. He imagined a rose-hued porpoise sitting next to Maple in the classroom, assembling puzzle pieces with her until they'd formed the solar system.

"A pink dolphin?"

"Swimming in the cove."

Ben knew the preschool's playground butted up against the water. But the cove was too far inland, so many miles from sea, no place for a dolphin to reside.

"Maybe it was a raft. Someone's lost inner tube."

"A pink dolphin. Miss Griffith said so."

Ben glanced at Maple in the rearview again. If her teacher said so, that settled things! Ben looked away, thought of Grace, imagined her sipping daiquiris by a poolside while her daughter slowly unraveled. He turned left onto their street, so hard Maple's backpack rolled off the seat and she burst into tears that he'd smashed Harriet's petals.

Ben chopped celery and garlic for dinner, then onions, eyes tearing while the evening news blared from the living room. After he put Maple to bed, he would find her—he would search and search until he found Grace, her new telephone number, no lines disconnected and no posted letters to return.

"There he is, Daddy."

Maple's voice came from the sofa, where she sat cradling the ghost in her arms. He peered over the sofa to the television, where a news reporter stood at the edge of Herring Bay Cove, a splash of coral skin in the water behind her.

"Well, there you have it." The reporter smiled, teeth flashing white as bleached plastic. "We can't say why he's here, or even where he came from. But the little guy appears to be an albino, and he seems to be here to stay."

Maple stood up on the couch. "What's albino?"

Ben stared at the television, then at his daughter holding her Mason jar, its contents as impossible as the pink dolphin on TV. He set the chopping knife down, moved into the living room, and sat on the sofa.

"It's when the body doesn't produce any melanin pigment at all." He looked at Maple. "Melanin gives our body color."

"But the dolphin's pink. He has color."

"Some forms of albinism produce a pink color. All over."

Maple peered into the Mason jar. "Could Harriet be albino?"

"I don't know." Ben sighed. "She'll have to tell you herself."

When he tucked her into bed, Harriet's ghost presiding over them from the nightstand, Maple looked up at him, her features cracked with sorrow.

"What color is the dolphin's heart?"

Ben didn't understand. He asked what she meant.

"Is his heart colorless too?"

Ben laughed, and the lines of worry on Maple's face melted away and she began to laugh too, and soon they were both giggling so hard it hurt. The sound pierced a dull ache into the center of Ben's chest. He felt the wish inside him then, just for a moment, for his own jar to keep. Not for ghosts, not daffodils, but for the sound alone—to hold his daughter's laughter in a Mason jar, to bottle and store, to set on his nightstand like fireflies, to hold light to the black.

At work and at night, Ben promised that he would keep the promise. He would not track down Grace, his research would not stray her way, he would not look for her nor think of her. This resolution, it felt good, since he knew now, tall fire burned to ember, that his anger was fading, replaced by some slow wash of grief, and he thought of Maple from his office at work, wondered when it would be right to bring up her mother.

After dinner, Ben sat reading on the sofa while Maple watched cartoons on the carpet, clasping Harriet's jar between her palms. She turned and looked at Ben, then left the living room and came back with a giant afghan from the cedar box.

"Let's make a fort."

Ben set his book on the coffee table. An animated mouse screeched on the TV.

"What makes you feel like doing that, sweet pea?"

Only Grace had ever built blanket forts with Maple.

Maple turned away and grabbed another blanket from the cedar box, and Ben didn't ask again, just pulled blankets over the couches.

When they at last sat inside their fort, a knitted halo of colors and yarn above, Ben lay on his back looking up, hands behind his head. Maple folded herself into a pretzel, rolled the Mason jar over the carpet.

"Harriet told me she misses the sun."

Ben sat quiet, placed a hand on his daughter's hair.

"She said ghost flowers have trouble. Getting the sun they need."

Ben studied the knitted patterns of the blankets surrounding them. Maple shifted beside him, set the jar upright, held it close to her chest.

"Miss Griffith said the pink dolphin's a baby."

"She's right. I saw that on the news today."

Maple rolled onto her belly, slumped her face into Ben's shirt.

"Miss Griffith said the baby's lost."

Her voice came muffled through the fabric, and she was quiet for a long time. Ben moved his arms to reposition her, but she held her face buried in his shirt.

"Miss Griffith said the mama's somewhere out to sea."

Ben turned toward his daughter but she curled away from him; he felt her breathing heavy through the fabric of his shirt. He put a hand on her small shoulder, over which he could see her rolling the Mason jar away and back, away and back.

He thought of Grace, that despite the coldness of the way she'd left, she always knew the rites of handling scraped knees, broken toys. He'd never considered himself good at that part of parenting, and now the strange shade of his daughter's emotions pooled out before him, unfamiliar hue, some foreign palette he had no words to name.

"Things will be better, sweetheart."

It was all he could think to say.

After she finally fell asleep and Ben carried her up to bed, he lay on the couch watching television, imagining Grace instead. He considered her puzzling temperament, complicated makeup—what strands of DNA could make a mother go, and if the same genes that stained dolphins pink could drain every shade from the human heart.

He rolled onto his side, flipped off the television, closed his eyes.

After brushing his teeth, Ben moved down the hallway toward his bedroom, turned into his office instead. He turned on the computer, mouse hovering above his search program, above every tool he would need to find her, to recover some combination of numbers—an address, a telephone—some code cracked to bring her home. But he sat paralyzed instead, the screen staring back at him, the computer's low hum filling the hollowed silence of the room.

Ben took a breath. His hands moved, opened a blank document instead.

He missed her. Beyond strands of genes or color or cells, he missed her, the imprint of her shape beside his, the tangerine smell of her hair, the way her hands sometimes rested absently against Maple's curls while Maple watched television on the couch, while Grace read a book. He missed her as Maple did, separate hurt, but in the end no different at all. Grace had been theirs, was now in some state of becoming, unfurling to not theirs, not anymore, all the things love became when heat paled to ash.

Ben stared at the screen, as white and unbroken as the life Grace imagined ahead.

YOU WERE:
The crack of bat against ball.
The first splash of crocus, poking through snow.
Mine. For only a moment.

At work, Ben threw himself into reports. He closed his office door, completed six reports in two days, trawling property values and political donations and asset wealth and corporation filings until he dropped all six reports on his boss's desk, leaving the office relaxed for the first time in weeks. Ben drove the length of streets toward Maple's preschool, windows down amid the noise of Friday traffic, of weekends starting early, but the breeze off the cove carried salt and sea into the car and Ben felt calm, a lulling center of grounded gravity, and he thought of Maple, that he would take her for ice cream after dinner.

But when he pulled up to the preschool, cars filled the parking lot—far more cars than there were children in the school, and Ben noticed news vans among the cars, antennas spiraling toward the sky. He parked across the street, walked warily toward the parking lot, and noticed a throng of cameras, of people crowded around the cove. Then he noticed the fishing nets, and Miss Griffith looking on from the schoolyard, a lone pine standing, the scattered cones of preschoolers dotted around her.

Ben saw Maple then, standing near the hem of Miss Griffith's dress—backpack strapped to her shoulders like a turtle shell, Mason jar clutched between hands, her eyes fixed on the cove where, when Ben followed her line of sight, the pink dolphin swam in furious circles while several fishermen surrounded him in small boats, dropped nets into the water from their decks.

"They're trying to capture him," Miss Griffith said, when Ben reached the schoolyard fence. "They're trying to bring him back to sea."

Maple looked up at Ben, moved to his side and leaned into his pant leg. He placed his palm on her head, curls of hair atop her sullen face, and looked out toward the water where the town fishermen tried again and again to drop their nets over the baby.

The dolphin swam in tight rings, pink skin brilliant above the cloud-darkened water. Ben knew, from a PBS special he'd once seen, that the dolphin ear hears things a human ear never would. That their range is eight times the capacity of the human auditory system, their lower jawbone a conductor of sound through the thickness of water. Ben watched the pink dolphin, frenzied circles growing tighter. The cameras, the reporters, the nets slapping the water's surface—the sound must have been unimaginable beneath the cove, echoed and magnified by the incomparable silence of the sea.

Maple's fingers pressed into Ben's leg, and he looked down to where she clutched his calf with one hand, the Mason jar with the other. They watched the nets descend, again and again until at last they landed upon the dolphin, compressed to near-stasis in whirlwind circling, and enclosed him in a webbed pocket. Maple turned away as the dolphin thrashed against the roped lattice, as the fishermen pulled the bundle close to the dock, securing the nets against wooden pillars until morning, when daylight would provide safer transfer. The dolphin pushed against the surface and then finally sank down into the net, submerged somewhere below the dock, pink skin glowing in the sky's darkening light.

The crowd began to disperse, and as Ben belted Maple into the backseat he thought of the dolphin, cowering crimson beneath the docks, alone in the water, at least until morning. The town's sentiment was right, if not the act. If only such things could be forced. Beyond the cove lay a wide, blackened expanse of unsounded ocean, a mother dolphin Ben doubted fishermen could intuit or trace. Albino babies were born from pigmented mothers all the time. There would be no pink beacon, no coral glow beneath the water, no trail of eerie light, submerged borealis streaking the ocean floor. Ben keyed the ignition, pulled away from the school. He knew they would never find her.

At home, Maple hopped up the stairs while Ben set to making dinner. Something familiar, something Maple loved, to cheer her, to leave room for ice cream. But when the eggs and waffles were made—breakfast for dinner, a surefire win—Ben called up the stairs to his daughter, and on the third summon she still didn't answer.

Ben skipped the stairs, two at a time, and moved down the hallway to Maple's room, empty. He searched the bathroom, the office, his bedroom, the closets. Then he stopped, turned back to her room, and looked past her bed to the floor near her nightstand, where Harriet's Mason jar stood alone on the carpet, just beyond the dust ruffle of Maple's bed.

Ben crouched on hands and knees, lifted the dust ruffle and peeked beneath the box springs. Maple lay there on her belly, cheek smushed against the floor.

"Harriet's sick." She turned her head away from him. "There's not enough sun. She's lost her yellow."

Ben looked back at the Mason jar, abandoned and empty. Then he compressed himself as thin as he could and crawled beneath the bed to lay flat beside his daughter.

He said nothing, just lay there next to her, watched her back rise and fall, steady wave of lungs. There was something calming in it, the simple fact of breathing, and he reached out his hand, held his daughter's in his.

"There might still be hope for Harriet."

Maple puffed air into her cheeks, didn't respond.

"Honey, maybe Harriet just needs to be outside. Maybe some sunshine will bring back her color."

Maple turned her head toward him, curls rustling against the box springs.

"Why did they trap the dolphin?"

Ben knew she'd heard Miss Griffith say why. He repeated the reason anyway. Maple's face crumpled into a pucker, and she pulled her hand away.

"But why do they need to trap him?"

Her voice was loud, then her features softened and she scooted away.

"Why doesn't the mama just come back and find him?" she whispered, and Ben's breath caught in his throat, simple act turned intolerable, some malfunction splintered from helix, their coded strands unraveling.

"Sometimes, the mothers, they—" He started, then stopped.

MOTHERS:
Abandon their children.
Leave their babies vulnerable.
Don't come back to find them. In coves, under beds.

Ben lay silent. There was nothing else to say.

"Maybe she lost her way, too," he said. An allotted honesty, the only one there was.

Maple lay there, quiet. A dust bunny floated toward her hair.

Ben felt the hardwood floor below him, pushing hard against his chest. He let himself lay still, alongside his daughter there beneath the bed, two boats in separate harbors. Then he moved toward Maple and clasped her shoulder, and when she didn't resist, he drew her gently along the floor until they both emerged from the dust ruffle.

Ben pulled his daughter into his lap, and they sat there against the bed, near the foot of Maple's nightstand, the jar empty beside them. Then Ben led her downstairs for dinner, for waffles and later for ice cream, and when he tucked her into bed he placed the Mason jar in the flower box outside Maple's window, for Harriet to soak in what light the pale moon could shed.

Ben awoke to the dim shade of a darkened bedroom, curtains not yet bright with the first hues of dawn. He headed downstairs anyway, brewed coffee, turned on the early morning news. The forecast, a day of sunshine. A good day to take Maple to the park, just enough wind for kites.

Ben turned from the coffee pot mid-pour when he heard mention of the pink dolphin. Newscasters, not yet on-site, reported that fishermen would transport the netted dolphin to the sea, sometime late morning, for safe release back to the ocean. Ben set his mug down. He glanced up the stairs toward Maple's bedroom. He knew, somewhere in the casing of his chest, that this was borne of good intention. But as he watched footage of the dolphin onscreen, swimming those furious pink circles before the nets descended, the core beneath the casing burned, some molten-hot hub inside a dull, rounded ache.

Ben grabbed a kitchen knife, pulled on his jacket, ran up the stairs to Maple's door.

"Wake up, sweetheart." Ben shook the shape beneath the rumpled sheets. "We're taking a little trip."

Maple stirred, rubbed her eyes.

"Can we take Harriet?"

In the car, as they pulled away from the driveway, headlights slicing into a day too new for sun, Ben turned on the radio, kept an ear to the news. Maple sat in her car seat, gazing out the side window, Harriet's jar rolling over the nightgown on her lap. Ben glanced at his daughter in the rearview every so often, considered the hazards of this plan. Dolphin freed by single father! Daughter taken by Child Services! Ben imagined the headlines, looked away, drove steadily toward to the cove.

But when they pulled into the preschool lot, there was nothing but calm, just the quiet lapping of water beside the seawall, and the slow marbling of sky as dawn approached, staining its path lilac. Ben unbuckled Maple from the backseat, then led her by the hand out to the edge of the dock. He knelt down near the nets, while Maple stood behind him watching, holding Harriet in her hands. The water rippled black in the absence of light, but as Ben watched, a pale shadow began to surface. Maple leaned in and watched as the dolphin slowly floated to the rough edges of the net, pink nose poking from the water, as if welcoming their presence. Ben knelt down, held his hand against the surface of the water. The dolphin pushed his nose against Ben's hand, rubber skin through roughened mesh. And as the dolphin sank again, Ben clasped his hand through the netting and held it, pulled the knife from his pocket with the other.

He told Maple to stand back. He clutched the knife and dragged it across the netting, at first tenderly, then more forcefully as the knife sawed through fiber after fiber until the strands began to unravel and break. The dolphin rose up again, coral shadow emerging from the deepest end of his allotted space, stayed close to the surface, curious. Ben sawed a small hole in the netting, then larger and larger as the binding tore and uncoiled, until at last a full-scale slit lined the net, a tear large enough for escape.

Ben sat back on his knees, held the knife limp against the dock. Maple peered at the water over his shoulder, and as they both watched, the dolphin hesitated, nosing the new opening. Then he pushed through the hole and disappeared.

They sat silent, breathing, an undulation matching the waves, the only living sound between sky and sea. Clouds stretched in wisps overhead, tinged golden, edges lined in lucent, growing light.

"Where did he go?" Maple asked, holding the Mason jar against her nightgown.

Ben watched the water for some spout or surfacing, without an answer. Beyond knives, netting cut, beyond the simple act of freeing, Ben knew he hadn't considered what next, what then for this dolphin, what if he simply swam around the cove, as he had been for days, to be captured once more by clueless fishermen by the time night fell again.

But then a gust of water burst forth, a flash of coral fin carved the surface near the mouth of the cove. The mouth led to the sound, and the sound led to the sea. The pink dolphin appeared to be headed that way, as if the harm of net was all the cove would be now, safe harbor no longer safe.

Maple watched the dolphin move away, eyes brimming beneath the first streaks of light. Then, before Ben could catch her by her nightgown's hem, she took off running down the dock, along the edge of the seawall.

Ben ran after her, ready to stop her, until he saw her holding out the Mason jar, held high above her as she ran, held out toward the sea. Ben slowed and let her go, kept a close distance in case she tripped or fell, but hung back, let her run. Ben watched as her short legs carried her to the edge of the seawall, where the mouth met the sound, where she crouched down and peered into the water. The dolphin had gone back under but Maple watched the surface, waves catching the first glints of dawn, until the coral skin reappeared.

The pink dolphin idled in the water, there by the edge of the seawall, appeared to be regarding Maple. As Ben watched, his daughter looked from the dolphin to her hands, then unscrewed the lid of Harriet's jar and emptied the empty contents into the water.

Ben's breath formed a knot inside his throat, a failure of coded function. The dolphin lifted his head to Maple, and Ben watched the pink blaze brilliant beneath the sun's first rays, some stretch of DNA burned as scarlet as his own, as his daughter held out her hands.

Ben stood still. You are, he thought. *YOU ARE:* —but nothing followed, nothing readily came. There was nothing but her. Nothing but what she was, no similes, no guesswork, no approximations. There was only his daughter, code stamped indelibly, within every strand of cells.

Maple screwed the lid on the Mason jar, turned away from the water, came and stood next to Ben. "What if he doesn't know where to go?"

"He'll find a way."

"Harriet will do better outside." Maple looked out toward the sound, set the Mason jar on the concrete. "In case she decides to come back."

Ben thought of Grace then, a disembodied thought, her location, her whereabouts as unimaginable as ghosts. He felt his daughter's hair, solid substance of her curls. He knew they should leave, head home and away from this place, before camera crews, fishermen, crowds reappeared. But he felt himself grounded in the breaking light alongside his daughter, no past and no prospect, only this, only theirs. Maple reached up her hand, slid her palm into his as the dolphin hesitated near the seawall then ducked quietly beneath the surface, disappearing into the sea.

UNTIL OUR SHADOWS CLAIM US

The first night he took one of us, the Challenger disintegrated over the Atlantic Ocean. We'd watched that day from our second-grade classroom at Rosewood Elementary, from the huddled space of the magic carpet where Mrs. Levy read to us during storytime, where she pulled the television close to the carpet's edge and dimmed the lights, like the movies, the launch as magic as the storybooks. We watched for all of them, especially for the teacher up there in space, and when the shuttle exploded only seventy-three seconds into flight, when Mrs. Levy held a hand to her mouth and shut off the television, we knew only that something had gone wrong, that the light bursting onscreen was not the same heart-fluttered spark of fireworks, the only other flare we knew.

At home, our parents watched the coverage. We watched with them, over TV dinners, over glasses of milk. We knew something terrible had happened, though we weren't sure what, and we felt sad and somehow empty until our parents tucked us into bed, into blankets soft and warm, and then we were safe again until we woke and heard other news while our parents poured our cereal and listened, a disaster of another kind, a tragedy far closer to home.

Craig Davenport, who'd sat next to us on the magic carpet, who'd played hopscotch and kickball on the playground with us, who at lunch had traded his juice box for our fruit snacks—gone, taken in the night from his own bedroom, the window still open when his parents came to wake him and found an empty bed.

There were speculations, notice of a vehicle, a number to call if any information was found. There were our parents, holding us close, dropping us off at the doors to school, watching us walk inside.

But we knew, as sure as we knew the shape of the letters that spelled our names, that at last he'd come for us, that what we'd done had brought all of this on.

We'd conjured him on the playground, bright blue October, our sweaters soft as fleece, a down barrier between our skin and the cold metal of rungs and bars. We crowded inside the rocket, tall structure painted the colors of our American flag, its diameter large enough to encase all of us, all clustered around a discarded piece of mirror that Tom Davies found in the wood chips nestling the swing set. Tom looked at each of us, fear scratched into the soft creases of his face, and told us of the Rosewood Phantom, the first time we'd heard the name, the first time the words stained the ridges of our tongues.

Tom told us Rosewood had a killer, many years ago, a man who stole the town's children one by one, any child who dared to step outside after nightfall, and at times even children tucked soundly in their beds. Tom told us the townspeople finally caught him, tortured him, wrapped him in a winding sheet; then they buried him alive beneath the hills of Stillwater Park, a death as terrible as all those parents' grief.

Tom paused, shifted his gaze around the perimeter of the rocket, said the story never ended there. He told us the Rosewood Phantom would appear if we said his name three times into a mirror, even into a broken shard neglected among wood chips. He said the Phantom would manifest in rags, bloodied remnants of the winding sheet, to take the souls of more children, to exact revenge on our town. When Rachel Vasquez said *That's a lie, that sounds just like Bloody Mary*, a game her sister played that never worked, Tom glared across all of us, told us he'd tried summoning the Rosewood Phantom once with his babysitter, in the bathroom of his basement. He said they'd never even made it to three, that upon the second summon the mirror began to shake, an eerie wobbling that forced the babysitter to turn on the lights, to make him promise he'd never tell his parents. Weeks later, when Tom lost a tooth and spat red into the bathroom sink, he left a dark stain across the porcelain, a stain that all his mother's scrubbing never lightened, a harrowing reminder of the Phantom's blood-stained rags.

I don't believe you, Nick Dorsey said. Nick, who never believed anything, who'd shouted that pigs and spiders couldn't talk when Mrs. Levy tried to read us *Charlotte's Web*, who'd told us all last year that Santa wasn't real, though most of us still believed. Nick reached into the huddle and grabbed the shard of mirror. Before Tom or any of us thought to stop him, he chanted the name of the Rosewood Phantom three times.

We waited, our breath all held as one. The wind picked up, blew yellowed leaves across the playground. We could have been angry with Nick, but none of us were, those few moments of waiting as delicious as sugar. And then nothing happened but the sound of a faint scream, carried across the blacktop on the autumn wind, a lone call of triumph from the four-square grids.

Nick threw the mirror down, called Tom's bluff, told us ghost stories were for babies. Then we heard the whistle blown from the school doors, the end of recess, and we climbed down from the rocket, disbanded our summit, left the mirror shard abandoned inside the rocket's cage. And then three months later Craig Davenport disappeared, and a real rocket broke apart.

These were links, impossible to discard, as we'd so carelessly done with the mirror.

Spring arrived early, melted the icicles from the tree limbs beyond our windows, pushed a space between us and our nation's lost rocket, and even helped us forget the empty desk in Mrs. Levy's classroom, Craig's pencil box still inside, a sign of hope to all of us that he'd come back someday for its contents, that he'd sit beside us again. We moved through Valentine's Day, the first real reminder that Craig was gone—our shoeboxes papered and glittered as mailboxes for valentines, for the cards we brought each member of the class, even Craig, a puffy painted box Misty Jones had made for him that sat atop his desk, its mail slot overflowing. But then an early wave of warmth drove the snow away, drove the weight of Craig from our minds occupied instead by lighter coats, by splashed puddles and mud, until the thaw brought forth police, as readily as it drew small crocuses and ants.

On our broadcasts, new searches—a new thirst for clues, hidden all those weeks beneath hard-packed snow; new locations to inspect, new community volunteers prepared to slug through sodden forests, to dig beneath softened ground. Our parents asked us, at times, if we remembered anything particular about Craig, if we'd seen anything unusual that day. We shook our heads no, avoided our parents' eyes, and on the playground avoided the rocket.

Mr. Tillman, one of Craig's neighbors, had reported seeing a strange vehicle on their street that day, 1979 Buick LeSabre Estate, a brown station wagon he'd never seen before, parked along the mailboxes that afternoon while he watched daytime game shows. The police followed that lead, though that was all we knew, and no other clues presented themselves under layers of snow, finally melted. While our town picked up searching we receded, kept our mouths shut, and at night locked our windows tight, crouched beneath covers, waited for the turn of doorknobs, the creak of panes slowly rising.

But nothing came, no telltale sounds, not even brief glimmers in mirrors though we held our breath every time we brushed our teeth. And then March melted into April, and no more clues were found or pursued, and early spring slid into full bloom, tulips and hyacinth lightening us, relaxing the tight cores of our chests, settling us into sleep as their growing bulbs guarded our yards.

And then in late April, the day after the Chernobyl disaster, after we learned that over four thousand people had been killed, a radioactive bloom above two continents, we awoke to a world tilted even further off its axis, a world in which Rachel Vasquez had disappeared.

As the police swarmed our school and streets, as our parents spread their hearts between the Ukraine and Rosewood, disasters separated by seas, we knew for sure that there were no misgivings, no coincidences. We knew what we'd done, and we knew the scope now, unfathomable. We'd brought these disasters upon ourselves, and upon the world as well. We'd taken two of our peers from their parents, with imprudence born of curiosity and nothing else, and now the stakes had risen beyond the height charts lining our closet doors: looming ghost, the deaths of more people than we knew to name.

Our parents installed security systems, new technology, Rachel taken from her bedroom just like Craig. They bought us personal alarms, tucked mace inside our pockets, an arsenal of protections that we knew, even as we accepted them, could never save us, neither siren nor latch, not the tightest of bolts tugging our windows shut. We were not safe, none of us, and we curled into ourselves, grew quieter as the police descended, tried relentlessly to determine what connected Craig and Rachel, why Rosewood, why this class and these kids?

Tom Davies began collecting meteors, though we all recognized their shapes as shale. We watched him scour the playground, line space rock along his desk, where he'd watch them for hours, ignoring Mrs. Levy and imagining, we were sure, another world beyond this one, a planet of gentler tilt. Karen Kettleman stood at the edge of the swing set during recess, stared at the sun long enough to brand an afterimage into her brain, some vision that flashed long after she closed her eyes, something bright and burning. And Nick Dorsey pored over *Two-Minute Mysteries*, as if solving them might open a portal, some solution, as if knowing how Mr. Deeds died could dissolve the impossible specter of death.

When Trina Johnson's personal alarm went off in her backpack, a blaring sound that interrupted Mrs. Levy's storytime and took over five minutes to stop while the siren blasted ever louder, splitting our ears, Tom at last signaled to us, every one of us across the magic carpet, somehow less magical now, with a flicker of eyes we knew not to ignore. In the library, when we should have been finding books for our annual readathon, we met by the card catalogue instead, flipped through musty entries until we found the Rs, then Rosewood, then the Rosewood Phantom at last. We holed away in a deserted corner, behind young adult stacks where the windows leaked in faint light, and scanned our books, only two on all of Rosewood, until we found the paragraphs we needed, the Phantom himself.

What we found sank our hearts, so little information for so much hurt. His name, unknown. Lost over time, like every name in the Ukraine that we didn't know, never would. All those parents, also lost, not even brief mention of a winding sheet, not the rags Tom promised would appear. The only mention we could find was of a killer, that he'd existed, that he'd been buried in Stillwater Park like Tom said. But the legend—just a story, a tale to keep children from wandering off after dark, with no word or warning of perfect sunshine, of the shade we'd brought in light.

Tom sat back on his heels, held his palms against his jeans. *I told you there'd be nothing*, said Nick, not believing, even still, though his voice cracked against the syllables, opened a gap of doubt. He waited, hovering with the rest of us, over books that told us nothing, though we lingered, as if the black text below us might rearrange itself into the absolution we craved.

The police trekked through our neighborhoods, made maps, made diagrams. They tracked every Buick LeSabre Estate, every color, every year, every driver. They hunted yards and forests, swollen by rain and spring, scoured sodden landscapes for footprints, for hairs and blanket fibers and clothes. In early May, our local broadcasts erupted for several days when Officer Franks found a bloodied rag in Craig's yard, discarded beneath Mrs. Davenport's rosebushes. We lay hiding in our beds, not sleeping, strange roil of shame and hope and fear, that the rags were what we'd waited for, that this was the end, that one of us, we weren't sure who, would have to start talking.

We hoped for an end as much as we feared it—that blood meant our classmates were not simply elsewhere, but gone. We imagined limbs, broken or worse. We imagined teeth, sharp nails, cloths to cloak and suffocate. We imagined the crushing sensation of hands, clamped down on our chests while we slept, pulling us away, beyond windows, beyond the walls of our rooms, and though some of us had never known religion we prayed, beside our beds at night after we heard our parents settle into sleep, that the Phantom was found, that he'd never find us.

But our salvation, some exhaled breath that lifted this from our shoulders, never came. We awoke to the morning news, only animal blood, a clue that still might have signaled a lead if not connected immediately to Jericho, Mrs. Feinberg's cat, a neighboring, pregnant feline who'd birthed her kittens beneath the Davenports' porch. The police had found one dead kitten near Mrs. Feinberg's sycamore tree, wrapped loosely in the rest of the bloodied rag, an attempt at burial by claw and teeth and Jericho still hiding beneath the porch, refusing to come out.

We imagined Craig's parents, in their home above this feline mother, equally sequestered, equally heartbroken. We felt the compression against our own rib cages, as those astronauts must have felt before they ever reached orbit, mistook for gravity, as every heart in the Ukraine must have felt at the blast, a weight as unimaginable as a phantom's pale hands, gripping the stalks of our necks.

The pulse of summer approaching soothed us, the days growing warmer, then warmer still until our final day of class had come and gone, celebrated with kickball and popsicles, with an outdoor field day and with lingering looks at our classroom, as we waved Mrs. Levy goodbye. Then we were on our own, no classmates and no carpet, no pencil boxes to remind us of what we'd lost. The trees thickened above us, and leaves erupted from their branches, a canopy of green light that grew steadily darker through June.

We spent our days splashing at the pool, guarding lemonade stands, thumbing through our summer reading lists, full sun beating above us, a light bright enough to erase the shade we'd shared. We felt our parents relax, calmed by sun, by warmth and no news on our television screens, and we stayed up late, had sleepovers, watched *Cujo* and *Carrie*, films we were still too young to see, films we couldn't help but watch. The thrill felt illicit, a transgression all the same, but this time one that felt honest, and our guilt slid away on the unending calm of each day. We had picnics with our families, chased ice cream trucks, helped our parents make sun tea, left on the back porch to steep in sunshine. We marveled at fireworks on the Fourth of July, let ourselves fall silent and hushed beneath the glare of their splendor, and for only a moment thought of the space shuttle's sparks, an unbearable trail of light dissolving into ember. But every night at dusk, when our neighborhood lights flooded on, we whipped home on our bikes, spokes whirring with wind, or we stayed home altogether, watched from our windows as the streetlamps flickered on. We could see them from our beds, pools of milky light on the sidewalk, illumined circles that at any moment we expected to break with a flash of shadow, a flutter of torn rags.

We knew the police were still looking. We watched their cars patrol past the pool, saw them stationed on our streets. But the long days, that lack of dark, let us forget the things we'd done, let us off the hook by keeping us from one another, no collective conscience, no reminders in the glances we shared, in looks we now avoided.

And then in August, our class lists posted, we walked with our parents to the school doors, felt a cored dread return. We saw our names listed together, heard our parents exclaim joy, tell us we'd move through third grade together, Mr. Jeffries's class, no longer Mrs. Levy's magic carpet but together all the same. The sun felt strange above us as we walked home, and we lay awake at night and felt summer receding, even in restless heat, in the stretch of weeks we still had until Labor Day.

Then in late August, full sun overhead, we awoke to an explosion of carbon dioxide in Cameroon, the unimaginable deaths of thousands of people, so much livestock; and to the disappearance of Nick Dorsey, gone before school even began.

We sat before televisions, forgot our bicycles, our books, our swimsuits. The Rosewood pool closed, off limits for safety until further notice, and the flash of blue and red lights beneath blistering sun, a heat that simmered against blacktop. We watched FBI agents fan through our community and saw reporters question our neighbors, interviews we watched on local broadcast and beyond, the disappearances swelled to national news.

We watched our televisions for Nick Dorsey, and for Rachel and Craig, but also for Cameroon, all those people, all those animals, a cloud of asphyxiation over Lake Nyos that we felt enclose our own throats, a constriction of lung and air sac and cell that made some of us wake in the night screaming, the flooded relief of gasped oxygen at once a reprieve, a requiem. That we could breathe, that we were alive. But that we awoke at all, to this world, a world no longer ours. We imagined suffocation, what that lack of breath might mean. We feared the shape of our own organs, that our lungs could fail us, that our hearts could sputter and cease, and that we held things beating inside of us, things we'd never fully understand, things we couldn't trust.

Our parents held us close. They made our beds, washed our dishes, sang us lullabies and read us bedtime stories, though we knew as well as they did that we were too old now. We felt them watching us, at times, while we pretended to sleep, never knowing if they watched us breathe out of love or if they watched the windows beyond our beds, standing guard for the threats pressed like palm prints against our panes.

The school year came, without our wanting, beyond sobered Labor Day celebrations, no barbecues or last swims. The pool remained closed, water draining slowly, a murky pond of still glass that caught leaves from shaken trees. Our neighborhoods and parks kept curfew—past dusk, no cookouts or bike rides, the streets deserted and silent. The FBI remained in Rosewood, stood guard outside our school, alongside police and parents and community volunteers, a wall of protection to keep us inside, to keep us safe. But our classroom no longer was, neither cocoon nor nest, not a place that felt sound with so many gone, so many missing. Mr. Jeffries welcomed us, had us glitter new nametags, arranged us in desk pods that were full, no missing desks, no vigil pencil boxes. But we knew, as he knew, a misgiving we heard beneath his voice, bright but clear, as he began his first lesson on life sciences, as he tried to ignore that we were those kids, from Mrs. Levy's class, those kids who were connected by inexplicable lines, by irrevocable bounds.

Misty Jones was the first to act out. During storytime, no magic carpet but a nook in the corner of the room, she stayed at her desk as we all moved to the corner, her face crumpled and red before she smashed her pencil box against her desk, its contents splintered and rattling. Mr. Jeffries looked up, rose from his rocking chair in the nook, but Misty was already gone, ran from the room and hid in the last bathroom stall until her father picked her up early. Then there was Karen Kettleman, who never came inside from recess, whom police were already tracking around the perimeter of school before they found her curled up inside the rocket, awake but unmoving, and shivering though the September sun still bore down bright above.

We all felt unhinged, though Mr. Jeffries tried his hardest to calm us, an effort that broke our hearts a little, as much as our parents' concern for us did, their worried glances we saw and ignored. We got into first fistfights, slammed each other against corridor walls, a solidity that felt satisfying. We remembered the sensation of fist against skin as we tried to fall asleep, held the feeling close against our fingertips, a memory of tangibility to beat back, to drown out the windowpanes beyond the foot of our beds.

We struggled together inside the confines of a classroom, that first week a preliminary taste, some terrible foreshadowing of what the year would bring, what we would force ourselves to endure. We longed for Nick's distrust, a trait we'd once hated but ached for now—some checked rationality, a voice to tell us this wasn't ours, this wasn't what we'd done. We ran our hands over cavernous absence, indelible as ink in the wooden swirls of our desks, lines we traced during lessons that never led back to Rachel, to Craig, though we peeked sometimes into Mrs. Levy's classroom, at their once-full desks, at the magic carpet of what we'd been.

And yet we still held hope, sputtering flame, a tiny spark captive inside hollowed marrow to protect from wind, extinguishing gusts, that there was more for us than this. At night, we watched the glowing stars glued against our ceilings and imagined life beyond this, somewhere older, a place where this would end, where we would unfurl like crocuses and begin anew.

But at the end of that first week, just four days into the school year, we learned that terrorists had grounded a plane in Pakistan, hijacked with 360 people on board, that twenty of those people had been killed. We learned that Trina Johnson had disappeared overnight, and our sputtering flame blew out.

We watched an anger erupt in Rosewood, a rage kept bottled for months. We watched Trina's father collapse on his porch during a press conference, watched the contours of his face bend with fury and sorrow. We watched community volunteers become vigilantes, grab guns dusted off from cellar gun cases, meant for hunting and shooting cans, pulled forth from storage to kill.

Beyond culpability, beyond hope, we felt something change, something imminent and menacing. A space shuttle, a radioactive cloud, an explosion of lake and gas—these were things no one had rendered, disasters without intent, all terrible, terrible accidents. But this, violent siege, a disaster more deliberate, more calculated, and coming on us so much faster, only two weeks between Nick and Trina's disappearances. We felt a heaviness span the Atlantic, blanket our chests, the fear of all those families, so much brutality, a mirror held up to our own. We felt the gravity of our own violence, of a chain set in motion and now of inertia, as crushing as a phantom's hovering presence, his shadow cast long across our homes, our bedrooms, as the September sun sank under its own heavy weight.

We couldn't avoid each other, not anymore. We couldn't ignore the shared burden of our actions and inactions, our classmates missing, the world around us collapsing, as much as we couldn't ignore our collective hope burned down, gasped away on a trail of unfathomable loss. So when during recess Tom Davies caught our eyes, each of us watching the others, we allowed ourselves to move wordlessly to the rocket, pulled by common, magnetic force. We crowded inside the structure's cage, our separate shadows pooled beneath the sun, melded darkly into one.

A familiar summit, an anniversary, where nearly a year ago we'd brought this on ourselves. The enclosed space of the rocket felt wistful, as if we were young again, as if we had a chance to take this back, to decide against speaking and summoning. But there was no Nick, no Rachel. There was no Trina, no Craig bent over mirror shards, friends we'd heedlessly traded for novelty, fleeting thrill. Tom looked as us, waiting, and Misty Jones blurted out, *We could dig him up, we could set him free.* We held our breath, a thought we'd all shared, but Tom said no, we'd be too obvious, with the police and FBI, volunteers swarming the streets. And Stillwater Park was closed at dusk, he said, due to curfew, and where would we find shovels? Would we have the strength to dig?

Tom watched us a moment, and we knew then that he'd formed a plan. I will have a party, he said. His birthday, two weeks away. We would all be invited, would share cake and ice cream, but when his parents went back upstairs, time alone he knew they'd grant us, we would gather in the basement bathroom. We would summon the Rosewood Phantom, just as he and his babysitter had done before, and we would at last close this portal, send him home and away from us forever.

When Tom finished speaking, none of us said a word. We felt relief, finally sensing closure, some schematic of structure to rein in chaos. But we were frightened, wordless in terror, of a specter we'd only imagined, one we'd seen in no more than fluttering curtains, in shape-shifting circles of pooled streetlight. *We have to do this*, Tom said, and we knew that he was right. We knew the word right, as well as we'd known it then, though knowing cleared no path for us, no well-worn route to mercy.

On the day of Tom's birthday party, our parents drove us willingly. A distraction, some flash of joy amid weeks of panic, and supervised, all of us in one place. We wore party hats, festive cones. We brought gifts, ate cake, not caring whether we garnered a corner piece or the middle, the amount of icing so trivial in the wake of our mission. We pinned tails on a donkey, we watched Tom open his gifts. We wondered whether his parents knew from Tom's lack of zeal for each gift opened, or if they assumed only the heavy shade of our classmates, missing, shared celebrations no longer shared, our sanctuary fractured and broken. When Tom finished opening gifts and asked if we could watch cartoons by ourselves, they didn't hesitate, moved upstairs, offered us the allocated solitude they must have guessed we needed.

When Tom heard the door to the basement shut, heard its click, he raised the volume on the television, gathered us into the bathroom, lit a candle and turned off the lights. The pitch dark startled us, no windows, no light, no sun, only a flame casting our faces in ethereal glow, illumining the outlines of the mirror and sink, Tom's bloodstain still darkening its edge.

We've come to summon you, Tom began, *to drive you back from where you came.* An introduction that felt forced, even to us, and some of us laughed, giggled into our hands, out of nervousness, we knew, not humor. Tom stepped in front, before all of us, leaned his face close to the mirror. The candle lit his face from beneath, like flashlights held under chins beside campfires, for ghost stories, a terror we longed for, something foreign and lost. Then Tom turned to us. *Say it with me,* he said. And though our hearts drummed anthems inside our chests, though our temples broke small beads of sweat, we stood as tall as we knew how, straightened our backs like we'd learned to do before scoliosis tests, like we'd done against height charts.

Karen Kettleman, the quietest, said it first. *Rosewood Phantom.* The words on her tongue ripped chills across our skin. But we said it with her, *Rosewood Phantom,* and thought of Craig, of Rachel, of Trina. We let go of their pencil boxes, their friendship bracelets, handed over our need for vigil, for memory. We thought of Nick and yearned for him the most, to tell us this legend was for children, that there was nothing to fear.

And then, as we watched, the mirror began to tremble. We watched Tom wince, for only a moment, and then he said it first, the second chant, the fugue of our voices all waterfalling behind him. We heard ourselves speak as the mirror vibrated and shook, and for once we felt weightless, our guilt floated and hovering, even among terror, the greatest we'd known, every fear we'd kept secret escaped and at hand.

The mirror rattled against the wall, a noise drowned out by cartoons beyond the bathroom, a muted blare that settled an ache inside our bones, to be there watching, to be there and not here. But we felt right, so feathered and light—not just for our classmates but for everyone, those astronauts, each plane passenger, every voice choked silent by poison cloud or bloom and we pushed the last summon from ourselves, for them and for all of us, *Rosewood Phantom, Rosewood Phantom, Rosewood Phantom.* We screamed it for what we'd done, for what we'd not done and for every life ahead of us, every disaster averted, for everyone we imagined, every moment big and beautiful and rolled out before us, unscripted. As we spoke, the mirror stopped shaking, and a fogged swirl appeared in the center. And then the candle blew out, quick eclipse, and Tom flicked on the lights and we stood together, all of us there, every one of us wild-eyed and breathless and still.

After the New Year, after we watched the ball drop with our parents, wishing the year goodbye in the quiet privacy of our hearts, a year we wished to never see again, the FBI caught a man in Illinois, 1979 Buick LeSabre Estate, his vehicle linked to Rosewood. They caught him in a motel with a nine-year-old girl—still alive, returned her to her parents—spread the news across Rosewood and across the whole nation, Rosewood killer caught, Rosewood terror laid to rest.

We grew up, in spite of ourselves. We never knew the stain of kidnap or murder again, not after that year; had classroom birthdays and Halloween costume parades, the same as every other kid. We graduated into junior high, then high school, bloomed inside the softness of first kisses, first dances, held each other awkwardly beneath banners and before photographers, made faltering steps to connect. We never spoke of the Rosewood Phantom again, grew apart gradually, beyond initially comparing what we saw, what we might never have seen. Tom Davies swore he saw torn rags. Misty Jones, the bloodied shape of a face. But we stopped talking altogether when the killer was caught, our fear still unsettled that we'd ever endure this again. Because even though our town celebrated, though the FBI, the police and volunteers disbanded, we wondered what no one else addressed, what our parents hushed us for, when we raised the question unasked.

Why wasn't that girl from Rosewood?

Every other child gone missing, all of our friends, every anguish we bore, all here. But not her. A question we knew our parents wondered too, at times, and the parents of Trina, of Craig, a closure they'd never find.

We grew up. We left ourselves behind. We built homecoming floats, earned our driver's licenses, attended proms though we held hidden the burn of our classmates who never grew with us, never bought their first cigarette packs, never held someone close inside a car, a kiss goodnight, never unloaded their suitcases in front of their college dorms, never waved their parents goodbye.

We see it from the other side, now, hold that heartbreak as close as our children, those of us who have them, who didn't turn away from the possibility of a grief so vast, who understand now what all those parents lost. We've survived the collapse of regimes, the collapse of buildings, shootings inside schools, disaster after disaster that we couldn't have prevented, couldn't have caused. We watch the news with feigned disinterest, and we tell no one of the dull throb that hides, always, beneath the bones that hold our hearts.

Because we are waiting, all of us, though we never speak to one another, though we never go home to Rosewood. We are waiting for our shadows to claim us, as we tuck in our children, as we watch the evening news, for a killer never caught, for a closure that we have never found. We are waiting for a phantom to come for us at last, to pry open our windows, to smother this immeasurable guilt.

MOLLUSK, MEMBRANE, HUMAN HEART

When Dr. Carver made his rounds, clipboard in hand to check every lab's progress, Walter held the eyedropper high, tended fastidiously to the octopus's dietary needs, and checked the aerators to ensure that enough oxygen passed over her eggs, a thousand small pearls beaded beneath her tentacles. Yet after Dr. Carver peered over his glasses, nodded stern approval, and closed the metal laboratory doors behind him, Walter set down the eyedropper and stared into the tank, sometimes curled himself into a ball with his kneecaps settled into his eye sockets, and tried to remember how the world felt in the womb.

The small female—which Walter had named Sedna, though he never spoke the name aloud—hung a laced cord of eggs along the ceiling of her lair, a makeshift cave of plastic and store-bought rocks, and splayed her tentacles across the roof to protect them, though Walter saw the satin globes anyway through the translucence of her suctioned feet. There were thousands of them, a caviar of test subjects, and

Walter knew Sedna would die once they were born. He'd tried to feed her, an eyedropper of sugar water, no substitute for crabs. She'd ingested one of her own arms instead, a behavior Walter knew was common among mothering octopuses but he regarded this as protest nonetheless, Sedna stretched thin across the roof of the cave.

What they'd done was wrong. Walter felt the wrong rattle in the marrow of his bones, standing there in the lowest reaches of the labs, hidden away where officials from the National Academy of Sciences would never find them. Up above, tanks upon tanks of zebra fish filled the labs, creatures within the realm of regulation—their capacity to breed in enormous numbers, their small, lucent bodies fertile for the type of research Dr. Carver wished to conduct. Cardiovascular disease, he'd told the Institutional Animal Care and Use Committee, all those zebra fish and their tiny glowing hearts, to further our understanding of the organ that sustains us. But within the anonymity of night, Dr. Carver had caught an octopus himself, had pulled Sedna from the wild-dark sea beyond the reaches of the labs and had locked her beneath the ground for Walter to oversee, for Walter to ignore the experimental regulations on octopuses, the laws mandating that no surgery be performed without anesthesia for their nearly infinite nerves.

We are groundbreakers, Dr. Carver had told Walter once as they locked up the lab. Any scientist can find a cure for heart disease, but we, we will find the origins of love.

Walter had let his eyes slide toward the tank, had disavowed any *we* Dr. Carver intended.

The complex nervous system, the neurons in their arms, their problem-solving capacities and their ability to find their way through mazes—for all of these reasons, Dr. Carver had said, octopuses were the perfect candidate for exposing the human mystery of love. In the neurons, the synapses, the brain activity blinking blue, he would find that love was nothing more than a firing of electrical impulses, a Petri dish of tangible chemistry.

We can eradicate divorce, Dr. Carver said. We can match synapses perfectly, brain to brain, no messy guesswork involved. He'd laughed and looked at Walter. Animals don't have feelings, and neither do we. It's all just biology, nothing more.

Walter peered over the edge of the tank, watched Sedna's tentacles creep along the edges of her cave, there beneath the wavering surface of the water. Dr. Carver fixated on the brain but ignored her multiple hearts, a cephalopod, one of the only organisms with more than one center. Walter imagined her three hearts pumping lucid blood, three hearts to sustain her weak body, to beat above her pearls of children, and to perish, when they were born into this world.

When the thousands of eggs hatched and Sedna withered away, weak and feeble, Dr. Carver told Walter to dispose of her down the laboratory toilet and separate the small octopuses into containers. Walter donned latex gloves, divided the babies with a fishnet, and placed them in bowls no bigger than baseballs, to be dispersed among the basement labs, to be overseen by other attendants and prepped for adulthood, for surgery without the costly expense of numbing agents. Walter did as he was told, kept a hundred fishbowls in his own lab to watch and aerate, but he slid Sedna into a plastic container and stowed her quietly inside his briefcase.

At home, Walter waited for Roseline to return from work before they stepped outside together, through the backyard to the frog pond, a saltwater remnant of the sea that once washed over the land. Roseline observed with solemn poise as Walter lowered the octopus into the water; she crouched down and patted Walter's shoulder as he watched Sedna float away, disappear.

A sad day, she said, as Sedna's tentacles receded, hovering on the water as if waving goodbye. It's a shame they die after childbirth.

Walter gritted his teeth and stared at the water.

You know, honey, you can quit. Roseline rubbed her palm across his shoulders. We don't need the money. At least, not that bad.

Walter touched her palm, pulled her hand across his chest. She knew everything about the animals, the zebra fish and octopuses, and now she knew what was illegal, what constituted his crimes.

I can't leave them. He sighed, breath rippling the water. God, it sounds so stupid, but I can't. All those eggs.

Walter thought of the marbled eggs, creatures balled inside their tiny wombs and unfurling into light, shiny billiard balls burst to mollusks, their tentacles stretched and splayed beyond their shells. Roseline's hand squeezed his, a language developed without words, a tongue they knew alone, the squeeze of the childless while babies bloomed all around them, a grip that breathed *I know*.

That man is a fool, she said. You do what you can. Those eggs, they're in no better hands.

And Walter squeezed her hand back but wondered, if only for a moment—he wondered what she saw when she looked at him, what pheromones and oxytocin swirled through her brain to blind her to the trespasses he allowed, the mistakes he sidled alongside, complicit.

———

As the baby octopuses grew, Walter fed them sugar water, pumped full of vitamins and antibodies that would mask the lack of crabs, provide the nutrients starfish could not. Walter prepared them, documented their growth and size for Dr. Carver, but in the quieter moments in the lab, between feedings and aeration, Walter settled into his chair and blinked at the small mollusks through their bowls.

Little suction cups, no bigger than pencil points. Tentacles waving, testing their own movement, a fluid blanket of only muscles, no bone, just the beak Walter imagined squeezing through small spaces, the only hard place on their whole jelly bodies. Some of the octopuses began shifting colors, from their mottled pearl to muted yellows and orange that blended into what, Walter didn't know, their shapes the only substance in a lab of metal and endless water.

One morning, as Walter held the eyedropper over the fishbowls, he accidentally squeezed three drops into one bowl instead of the regulated two, and watched as the tiny mollusk below him swelled in size and color, muted gray to bright green. Walter crouched low, examined the little octopus through the glass, a billowing emerald circling the bowl. The octopus punched the water with tiny tentacles, then floated down to the floor of the bowl and lay there, skin flushed back to gray.

Walter blinked at the octopus. He dropped another sugar droplet into the water. The mollusk pulsed key-lime green and leapt, then receded back to the color of rain.

Walter looked around the room.

In moments he held a small rock poised high, the same that had adorned Sedna's cave, and dropped it squarely into the bowl, a splashing meteor hurtling through the water. The octopus darted to the rounded edges, flattening itself against glass as the rock settled to the floor, and then turned the darkest red Walter had ever seen, angrier than poison oak.

Walter stood in the middle of the lab, surrounded by fishbowl upon fishbowl, a room full of snow-globed pods. He walked on tiptoe among the bowls, peering cautiously down into the stilled surfaces, and dropped another pebble here and there, breath held as helium within his lungs. But none of the other babies reacted; they simply darted away without changing shades, and Walter picked up the fishbowl with the irritable mollusk inside—faded pink, sliding back to blemished gray—and set him apart, placed his sphere of a home beneath the lamp on his desk.

As the baby octopuses matured, Dr. Carver rounded the labs, made notes in his charts, studied their small anatomies for the best angle of incision, the ripest points of entry into their developing, fertile brains. He drew diagrams, held them side by side, pointed to the vertical lobe of the octopus brain and murmured *yes*, hummed the word beneath his breath, trailed his finger from there to the amygdala sketched inside the human model, where he believed the ghost of love resided.

This must be it, he told Walter—the place that holds all those electrical impulses. Those firing synapses that tell you to buy your wife flowers, to do the dishes.

Dr. Carver laughed, a wheezing cough. Walter didn't know anything about Dr. Carver's personal life or marriage, but he imagined something snarky and scornful, some relation full of contempt.

They are almost ready, Dr. Carver said. He stared at Walter through the glass of his spectacles. Are you ready for a windfall of press? Think of all the heartache we can prevent, the broken relationships we can thwart.

Walter nodded and looked away, and when Dr. Carver left the room, he pulled the fishbowl on his desk out from behind the lamp, his hiding place for the small octopus whenever the doctor entered.

In the weeks since Walter first set him aside, he'd watched the growing octopus shift through a spectacular rainbow of colors, an array that none of the other babies displayed. He turned banana yellow when Walter shined the lamplight above him, and pumpkin orange when Walter placed other fishbowls near him, tiny tentacles splayed against the glass. He even turned deep purple once, when Walter placed a handkerchief over the fishbowl and left him alone for two days.

Dr. Carver will operate soon, Walter told Roseline that night, over dinner plates filled with noodle stew. On Peabody too—he'll know the count of one hundred. I can't keep him hidden forever.

Peabody? Roseline blinked, noodles suspended on her fork.

Walter sighed. Our little shapeshifter.

You named him?

They were only three words, but he knew then what Roseline did. He'd become attached, just like Sedna, and like baby after baby until Roseline finally said enough, no more names and no more trying, we will just have to let this go.

Walter set down his fork. I don't know what to do.

You'll figure it out. Roseline touched his arm. I have faith in you.

Walter watched her across the table, that word *faith*, what it could possibly mean. He'd been as incapable of stopping the death of one lone octopus as he'd been an entire bevy of lost children, failed births. Walter stared into Roseline's eyes and strained to see their corneas, small retinas, what prism refracted the complicated ways that love bent and illumined itself, and how it looked from the other side, the impossible perspective of a heart not his own.

After Dr. Carver locked up the labs the next day, moseying past Walter's room to tell him he could head home, Walter flashed a spare key, said he'd lock up himself after finishing the day's notes. After the reverberations of the doctor's footfalls fell silent, Walter pulled a plastic bag from his briefcase—not unlike the ones he'd used as a child, to take goldfish home from fairs—and slipped Peabody inside, bright crimson through the tide of water, then a little red balloon circling the bag, irate in his new environment.

Walter strapped the bag into the passenger seat, too small for full protection by belt buckles, and glanced over at stoplights, a red cloud still blooming through the bag, as if Peabody held his breath in ruby-cheeked protest.

At home, Walter moved quickly to the frog pond, unable to wait for Roseline. He untied the plastic bag and unfolded its contents through the ripples of the shoreline, watched Peabody float a moment as if confused, tentacles stretched out into the strangeness of vast water. His color shifted quickly, cherry red to cobalt blue, and he zipped away into the water, so fast Walter thought his small organs might have seized beneath the weight of new surroundings, but then a fountain-like squirt shot up from the center of the pond, a spray from Peabody's tiny beak.

When Roseline at last came home, she found Walter squatting by the bank as the sun dropped behind the trees, the frogs beginning to croak.

Is that him? she asked, arm extended toward the pond's center, where an egg-sized flash of blue splashed playfully through the water.

That's him. Walter watched as two frogs kicked their way toward Peabody, curious.

Roseline sighed, and Walter wondered if she disapproved. But she stooped down beside him, troubled the water with her fingers.

You did a good thing.

Roseline rubbed his back and headed inside, and Walter watched the trees swallow the last of the sun, a death stained in streaks across the marbled, darkening sky.

Walter watched Peabody swim, mornings before work and some evenings beside Roseline, their mugs of tea steaming ghosts. Peabody grew quickly, no longer confined by the edges of fishbowls, and propelled himself around the pond, sometimes floating along the banks to absorb the last of the sun, and other times poking the frogs with wonder, tentacles pulsing lemon yellow when they responded and played.

One morning when Walter opened the doors of his lab, Dr. Carver stood inside, holding a needle over a fishbowl. He looked up for a moment, sharp tip poised above water, then pushed the needle slowly into the trembling octopus's head.

A dye injection, Dr. Carver said, pushing fluid through the syringe. It will color the brain so we see what we're operating on.

But they're not ready yet. Walter dropped his briefcase and stared at the small octopus, tentacles shuddering. They're still babies.

All the better. Dr. Carver pulled the needle from the fishbowl. Now we can see how love begins.

Walter stood, stuck to the floor tiles, while Dr. Carver moved around the lab prepping steel instruments, waiting for the dye to soak through cells. Walter stared at the eyedropper on his desk, a daily duty of care, inconsequential, meaningless now. Dr. Carver pulled the octopus, now immobile, from its tiny snow globe and pinned its tentacles to the bed of a Petri dish, filled with just enough water to keep it alive, the top of its head exposed to air.

Walter looked away when Dr. Carver made the first incision, an exactitude of scalpel through membrane and tissue. Without vocal cords there were no screams, but Walter imagined them anyway, piercing shrieks that percolated the nerve endings within his arms, spread down the length of his legs. He envisioned the vertical lobe that Dr. Carver penetrated, so close to the insular cortex—the center of pain for both humans and invertebrates, of unanaesthetized sensation, of heartbreak.

When Roseline walked through the front door that evening, Walter sat in an armchair, room dark, every light extinguished as dusk spread through the windows and across the floor.

He sacrificed an octopus today. Walter looked up at Roseline. This started too soon. They're still so young.

Walter felt a pressure then, some darkened cloud filling the space beneath his ribcage, ballooning through his lungs. He closed his eyes, blinked it back—what ineffable pain radiated on the shared wavelength of words, as if ejecting them into air was the only catalyst that made sorrow real.

You can't save them all. Roseline stood before him, bent down and touched his face. This isn't your fault.

Walter gazed at her cheeks, just shy of her eyes. He strained to see skin cells, blood coursing beneath them, the way they could brighten and stain her face red, when she laughed too hard, or when she lay flushed and still, just after they made love.

After dinner, as Walter scrubbed the dishes, he heard the back door open and bang shut, and found Roseline at the edge of the pond, hugging her sweater around herself, breath clouding in swirls. He watched as she threw shrimp in the water, pulled from the freezer inside, and let them thaw on the pond's ripples until Peabody pulled them under.

Walter stood beside her. Her shoulders came only to his chest.

Why do you love me?

She threw another shrimp. Because I do.

He considered this, what reason or logic might hide in three words, and stared out above the pond toward the pockmarks of stars, pinpoints letting in light. Walter felt blind, unable to see them, and closed his eyes where the dots of a thousand octopuses swam against black, all the particles of children that never were.

I am not a good man.

Walter opened his eyes and watched the water. He could not look at his wife. The doctors never said why, what mystery brought them here just to wash them away, but in the waiting room that last time he knew he'd failed her somehow, that maybe with another man, Roseline might have enfolded soft skin, tiny hands in her arms.

Roseline set down the shrimp. She turned so she was facing him.

You are the best of men.

Her voice filled his rib cage, rattling against bone. Peabody crept to the shore, extended a short tentacle, touched Roseline's ankle. She bent low and slid the remaining shrimp into the water, and as Walter watched her silhouette he yearned to know what was it that brought her such calm, this other half of marriage, this impenetrable wall that slid beneath the shade of the known world.

———

When Walter returned to the lab in the morning, Dr. Carver again stood near the fishbowls, suspended above them until he settled on one near the edge, plucked the rounded glass to transport onto the examination table.

I thought yesterday was a test. Walter watched Dr. Carver pull the octopus from the water, pin it roughly against Petri dish.

They're ready, Dr. Carver said. They've been ready a long time.

Walter tried, but could not look away. He watched as Dr. Carver pushed the last of the pins through the octopus's waving tentacles, their tips curling and recoiling, attempting movement, failing. He watched Dr. Carver slide the needle through tissue and push the syringe, saw the octopus squirm and flinch. He watched the steel knives and scalpels come out, lined up along the tray. And he watched Dr. Carver slice through skin and organ, plunging the scalpel deep into the vertical lobe, even as the octopus blinked and trembled.

Walter watched everything, stood motionless, waited until Dr. Carver at last pulled the scalpel free, until the octopus slumped unmoving and died.

You're a good man for observing. Dr. Carver snapped his latex gloves free, threw them in the trash can with the Petri dish. The more you pick up, the closer you'll be to making these incisions yourself.

Walter stared at him, imagined him driving home after work to what, he couldn't guess—the image stopped there, blank and clear as the vacant sea.

We'll get it right, don't you worry. Dr. Carver waved a hand over the rows of fishbowls. It's not like we don't have room for error.

He laughed, rough sandpaper, and slipped out the metal doors. Walter listened to his footsteps recede down the hallway, standing immobile before the lines of fishbowls, watching their fluttering shapes, tentacles undulating like banners through the fluid of their tanks.

Walter moved to the trash can, peeked over its edge. The Petri dish lay among the discarded gloves, biohazard waste, dirtied rags. Walter reached down and pulled the dish out, held the unresponsive octopus to his face, its limp body no bigger than a tiny, pale heart. Even without Peabody's colors, shades to expose joy or sorrow, Walter could see that the octopus had died in pain. No tint or hue was needed, no dye to stain what was evident, there inside the octopus's ashen tentacles, pallid suction cups. A center unknowable, one Dr. Carver would never find, the secrets of sea and land locked flush inside a safe, bolted tight.

Walter slid the Petri dish into a plastic bag, tucked it securely inside his briefcase. He stared toward the fishbowls, watched their silent small vibrations in the water, heard the hum of the laboratory refrigerators, the oscillating currents of the ventilation system.

Inside the laboratory closets, Walter found a stack of cardboard boxes, the same the fishbowls had arrived in. He laid them out on the floor, a hopscotch grid of boxes, then moved quickly to stow the fishbowls inside of them, covered with plastic wrap, packing tape, everything to transport them carefully away. He stacked them, one above the other, then steadied his briefcase on top, a tower of escape, of revolt.

He waited until he heard Dr. Carver move into another lab, then hurried down the hallway, out the laboratory doors to the sunshine, to the bedrock shelter of his car.

Through bumps and potholes, Walter heard the fishbowls rattle against one another, glass knocking glass inside his trunk. But he sped up anyway, moved hurriedly away from the laboratory until he'd at last arrived at home, threw open the trunk, and hastened the pile of boxes quickly around the house, through the backyard, toward the frog pond.

Dr. Carver had surely stopped by the lab by now. As he pushed open the backyard gate, Walter pictured how wide the doctor's eyes would be, the lab empty, all the fishbowls gone. He would lose his job, he knew. He would be fired, he would be free.

But when Walter reached the pond, he stopped short, feet planted, gaze frozen. The weight of the boxes pressed down into his arms and he set them down and felt his entire body collapse, all haste expelled. A blackbird called from somewhere above, some high branch or tree, disembodied, every noise and hum fractured, skewed impossibly from grass, from bark, from prickled air on skin.

There, in water once clear, floated hundreds of frogs, all dead, spots of color in a boundless pool of black. Emerald specks, points of light, a constellation made terrible, illumined by the night-dark torrents they drifted silently upon. Walter's eyes moved over the mess, over what could have possibly happened here, and he moved toward the shore, crouched down and touched the water.

His fingers came back black when he pulled them away. The shade stained the ridges, the patterns of his fingertips as ink would, ink for a lineup, ink for escape, for defense. Pure melanin, poisoning the water, ejected from ink sacs embedded inside Peabody's intestines, small pouches filled with enough toxin to destroy a whole sea of predators, if the right impetus provoked. Walter scanned the water, finding only frogs upon frogs, but then he squinted, out toward the center of the pond, toward some floating texture, a black matching the water's darkened midnight.

Walter stood, strained to see, and his whole body went limp, his eyes closed upon their own aim when he saw what was there. Peabody, lifeless and floating, stained as black and dark as the water, tentacles curled around the drifting body of his mother. And Sedna, preserved by the cold water, unearthed from the clouded mud of the pond floor that morning as Walter stood by to watch another octopus perish in the lab, as Peabody poked curious at the mud, as he searched for frogs at play, found his mother instead.

Walter sat upon a log, clasped his hands to his mouth. How stupid. He breathed, closed his eyes, remembered Sedna. What a careless mistake. How irresponsible, how reckless, how incautious he had been and now, all those frogs, Peabody's colors gone, so much black.

Walter opened his eyes, looked at the boxes. He imagined the baby octopuses, all ninety-nine of them, hovering and blinking in their bowls. He pictured all the other fishbowls still inside the lab, mollusks suspended in their small tanks, waiting. He stared out across the water. He held his head between his palms.

When Roseline came home, she found him still and silent on the log, head bent inside his hands, the boxes stacked against the shore, briefcase still perched precariously on top.

She stood, breath suspended, eyes pooling across the pond.

What happened?

Walter didn't look up, to hear her say again, *This isn't your fault*—he would shut it out and away until she met him eye to eye, until she finally breathed yes, you are not a good man, you are not the man I loved.

But she only sat beside him. She pushed her palm across his knee. Her sweater rustled against the log, caught on the rough edges of bark. Walter listened to her breathe in and out, lung membrane, air sacs, cells. He felt her heart pulse through her fingers, through his jeans, just one muscle-strapped core instead of three but beating hard all the same, strong, steady. All the eggs, all the frogs, all the mollusks and unborn children and here she was, her solid shape, all skin and cell that masked what she'd hide forever, some impenetrable core she held beneath bone.

What are we going to do?

Roseline's gaze swept the pond, the boxes, the frogs and floating dead.

We will do what we can.

Walter looked at her. He would fail, they would fail. Again and again. *You can't save them all*, and he knew that, though his chest burned to even think it, every egg, every cortex aching sorrow. He exhaled. He fell into her weight. He curled his fingers around her hand and held her, cupped in the shelter of his palm, a separate world to climb inside, to be theirs, to be known.

ACKNOWLEDGMENTS

The help, guidance, love, and support of so many people have gone into the creation of this book.

Thank you to the editors who first supported these stories: Caitlin McGuire at *Berkeley Fiction Review*, Jake Adam York at *Copper Nickel*, Steven J. McDermott at *Storyglossia*, Laura Benedict, Pinckney Benedict and Kevin Morgan Watson at Press 53, Robert James Russell and Jeff Pfaller at *Midwestern Gothic*, Andrew Scott and Victoria Barrett at *Freight Stories*, Beth Staples at *Hayden's Ferry Review*, Valerie Vogrin at *Sou'wester*, Chris Heavener at *Annalemma*, Stacy Bodziak at *Bellevue Literary Review*, Nick White and Alex Fabrizio at *The Journal*, Andrew Gray at *CutBank*, and Rebecca Morgan Frank and Barrett Bowlin at *Memorious*.

I am deeply indebted to the amazing team at Dzanc Books: Dan Wickett, Steven Gillis, Steven Seighman, Guy Intoci, Jeffery Gleaves, and Michelle Dotter. Thank you for everything, and for your support and faith in this book. It is truly a dream realized to work with each of you.

My gratitude will be lifelong for the group of colleagues, mentors, and friends at Bowling Green State University, who saw these stories in their earliest forms. Wendell Mayo, Theresa Williams, Lawrence Coates, and Michael Czyzniejewski: thank you for your instruction and close guidance. Megan Ayers, Alison Balaskovits, Matt Bell, Joe Celizic, Brad Felver, Dustin Hoffman, Brandon Jennings, Catherine Keefe, Stephanie Marker, Aimee Pogson, Jacqueline Vogtman, Jessica Vozel, Bess Winter, and Michelle Zuppa: thank you for your feedback and friendship. Thank you as well to Callista Buchen, Noah Buchen, Nikkita Cohoon, Ian Cohoon, Seth Fried, Brad Modlin, and Stokely Klasovsky. I am honored to know each of you, in perpetual awe of your talents and kindness, and forever grateful for our time in the long light of northern Ohio.

Thank you to the communities at the University of Utah and the University of Cincinnati for their continued support and dynamite talents. Thank you to Lareese Hall for informal workshops and inspiration. Thank you to Brittney Stone and her family, and to Molly Patterson and Marissa Rosen. I am lucky to have grown up with you.

Thank you to my extended family, to the loving memory of my grandparents, and to my new family, Jeff Heine and sweet Noa.

Thank you to my parents, Michael and Maureen, and to my sister, Michelle. There are no words, even if my life is a striving to find them. You are my foundation. Thank you for your unwavering love and support, your goodness, and for showing me every magic this world can hold.

Thank you to Josh Finnell, first reader, partner in wonder and the magic I found: you are my reason for everything.